TH

by Sandra Marton

In order to marry, they've got to gamble on love!

Welcome to the world of the wealthy
Las Vegas family the O'Connells.
Take Keir, Sean, Cullen, Fallon, Megan and
Briana in your hearts, as they begin that most
important of life's journeys—a search for
deep, passionate, all-enduring love.

Coming soon in Harlequin Presents™

THE SICILIAN MARRIAGE

Briana O'Connell thinks she prefers being
single. Gianni Firelli is certainly not the man
she dreams of. Gianni is gorgeous, but he's
also autocratic and demanding. Then Bree
learns that she has become guardian of a
six-month-old baby. Raising a child seems
daunting enough, but when Bree discovers
she holds joint guardianship with
Gianni Firelli—she's devastated!
Bree and Gianni will have to enter
into a marriage of convenience.

Available April 2005
#2458

Award-winning author **SANDRA MARTON** wrote her first novel while still in school. Her doting parents told her she'd be a writer someday and Sandra believed them. In high school and college, she wrote dark poetry nobody but her boyfriend understood. As a wife and mother, she devoted the little free time she had to writing murky short stories. Not even her boyfriend-turned-husband understood those. At last Sandra decided she wanted to write about real people. That didn't actually happen, because the heroes she created—and still creates—are larger than life, but both she and her readers around the world love them exactly that way. When she isn't at her computer, Sandra loves to bird-watch, walk in the woods and the desert, and travel. She can be as happy people-watching from a sidewalk café in Paris as she can be animal-watching in the forest behind her home in northeastern Connecticut. Her love for both worlds, the urban and the natural, is often reflected in her books.

You can write to Sandra Marton at P.O. Box 295, Storrs, Connecticut, U.S.A. (please enclose a self-addressed envelope and postage for reply) or visit her Web site at www.sandramarton.com.

Sandra Marton

THE ONE-NIGHT WIFE

The
O'CONNELLS

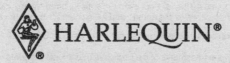

HARLEQUIN®

TORONTO • NEW YORK • LONDON
AMSTERDAM • PARIS • SYDNEY • HAMBURG
STOCKHOLM • ATHENS • TOKYO • MILAN • MADRID
PRAGUE • WARSAW • BUDAPEST • AUCKLAND

ISBN 0-373-12435-X

THE ONE-NIGHT WIFE

First North American Publication 2004.

Copyright © 2004 by Sandra Myles.

www.eHarlequin.com

Printed in U.S.A.

CHAPTER ONE

HE CAME INTO THE CASINO just before midnight, when the action was getting heavier.

Savannah had been watching for him, keeping her eyes on the arched entry that led from the white marble foyer to the high-stakes gaming room. She'd been afraid she might miss him.

What a foolish thought.

O'Connell was impossible to miss. He was, to put it bluntly, gorgeous.

"How will I recognize him?" she'd asked Alain.

He told her that O'Connell was tall, dark-haired and good-looking.

"There's an aura of money to him," he'd added. "You know what I mean, *chérie*. Sophistication." Smiling, he'd patted her cheek. "Trust me, Savannah. You'll know him right away."

But when she'd arrived an hour ago and stepped through the massive doors that led into the casino, she'd felt her heart sink.

Alain's description was meaningless. It fit half the men in the room.

The casino was situated on an island of pink sand and private estates in the Bahamas. Its membership was restricted to the wealthiest players in Europe, Asia and the Americas. All the men who frequented its tables were rich and urbane, and lots of them were handsome.

Savannah lifted her champagne flute to her lips and drank. Handsome didn't come close to describing Sean O'Connell.

How many men could raise the temperature just by standing still? This one could. She could almost feel the air begin to sizzle.

His arrival caused a stir. Covert glances directed at him from the men. Assessing ones from the women. Maybe not everybody would pick up signals that subtle, but catching nuances was Savannah's stock in trade.

Her success at card tables depended on it.

Tonight, so did the course of her life.

No. She didn't want to think about that. Years ago, when she was still fleecing tourists in New Orleans, she'd learned that the only way to win was to think of nothing but the cards. Empty her mind of everything but the spiel, the sucker and the speed of her hands.

Concentrate on the knowledge that she was the best.

The philosophy still worked. She'd gone from dealing three-card monte on street corners to playing baccarat and poker in elegant surroundings, but her approach to winning had not changed.

Concentrate. That was the key. Stay calm and be focused.

Tonight, that state of mind was taking longer to achieve.

Her hand trembled as she lifted her champagne flute to her mouth. The movement was nothing but a tic, a tremor of her little finger, but even that was too much. She wouldn't drink once she sat down at the poker table but if that tic should appear when she picked up her cards, O'Connell would notice. Like her, he'd have trained himself to read an opponent's body language.

His skills were legendary.

If you were a gambler, he was the man to beat.

If you were a woman, he was the man to bed.

Every woman in the room knew it. Too bad, Savannah

thought, and a little smile curved her mouth. Too bad, because on this hot Caribbean night, Sean O'Connell would belong only to her.

Again, she raised her glass. Her hand was steady this time. She took a little swallow of the chilled Cristal, just enough to cool her lips and throat, and went on watching him. There was little danger he'd see her: she'd chosen her spot carefully. From this alcove, she could observe without being observed.

She wanted the chance to look him over before she made her move.

Evidently, he was doing the same thing before choosing a table. He hadn't stirred; he was still standing in the arch between the foyer and the main room. It was, she thought with grudging admiration, a clever entrance. He'd stirred interest without doing a thing.

All those assessing glances from men stupidly eager to be his next victim. All those feline smiles from women eager for the same thing, though in a very different way.

Savannah the Gambler understood the men. When a player had a reputation like O'Connell's, you wanted to sit across the table from him and test yourself. Even if you lost, you could always drop word of the time you'd played him into casual conversation. *Oh,* you could say, *did I ever tell you about the time Sean O'Connell beat me with a pair of deuces even though I had jacks and sevens?*

That would get you attention.

But Savannah the Woman didn't understand those feminine smiles at all. She'd heard about O'Connell's reputation. How he went from one conquest to another. How he lost interest and walked away, leaving a trail of broken hearts behind him. Why set yourself up for that? Emotions were dangerous. They were impractical. Still, she had to admit that Sean O'Connell was eye candy.

He was six foot one, maybe two. He wore a black dinner jacket open over a black silk T-shirt and black trousers that emphasized his lean, muscular body. Dark-haired, as Alain had said. The color of midnight was more accurate.

Alain hadn't mentioned his eyes.

What color were they? Blue, she thought. She was too far away to be sure and, for an instant that passed as swiftly as a heartbeat, she let herself wonder what would happen if she crossed the marble floor, stopped right in front of him, looked into those eyes to see if they were the light blue of a tropical sea or the deeper blue of the mid-Pacific.

Savannah frowned and permitted herself another tiny sip of champagne.

She had a task to accomplish. The color of O'Connell's eyes didn't matter. What counted was what she knew of him, and how she would use that knowledge tonight.

He was considered one of the best gamblers in the world. Cool, unemotional, intelligent. He was also a man who couldn't resist a challenge, whether it was a card game or a beautiful woman.

That was why she was here tonight. Alain had sent her to lure O'Connell into a trap.

She'd never deliberately used her looks to entice a man into wanting to win her more than he wanted to win the game, to so bedazzle him that he'd forget the permutations and combinations, the immutable odds of the hand he held so that he'd lose.

It wasn't cheating. Not really. It was just a variation of the skill she'd developed back when she'd dealt three-card monte. Keep the sucker so fascinated by your patter and your fast-moving hands that he never noticed you'd palmed the queen and slipped in another king.

Tonight was different.

Tonight, she wanted the mark watching her, not her hands

or the cards. If the cards came the right way, she would win. If they didn't and she had to resort to showing a little more cleavage, so be it.

She'd do what she had to do.

The goal was to win. Win, completely. To defeat Sean O'Connell. Humiliate him with people watching. After she did that, she'd be free.

Free, Savannah thought, and felt her heart lift.

She could do it. She *had* to do it.

And she wanted to get started. All this waiting and watching was making her edgy. *Do something,* she thought. *Come on, O'Connell. Pick your table and let's start the dance.*

Well, she could always make the first move... No. Bad idea. He had to make it. She had to wait until he was ready.

He was still standing in the entryway. A waiter brought him a drink in a crystal glass. Bourbon, probably. Tennessee whiskey. It was all he drank, when he drank at all. Alain had given her that information, too. Her target was as American as she was, though he looked as if he'd been born into this sophisticated international setting.

He lifted the glass. Sipped at it as she had sipped at the champagne. He looked relaxed. Nerves? No. Not him. He was nerveless, or so they said, but surely his pulse was climbing as he came alive to the sights and sounds around him.

No one approached him. Alain had told her to expect that. They'd give him his space.

"People know not to push him," Alain had said. "He likes to think of himself as a lone wolf."

Wrong. O'Connell wasn't a wolf at all. He was a panther, dark and dangerous. Very dangerous, Savannah thought, and a frisson of excitement skipped through her blood.

She'd never seduced a panther until tonight. Even think-

ing about all that would entail, the danger of it, gave her a
rush. It *would* be dangerous; even Alain had admitted that.

"But you can do it, *chérie*," he'd told her. "Have I ever
misled you?"

He hadn't, not since the day they'd met. Lately, though,
his attitude toward her had changed. He looked at her differently, touched her hand differently...

No. She wouldn't think about that now. She had a task
to perform and she'd do it.

She would play poker with Sean O'Connell and make the
game a dance of seduction instead of a game of luck, skill
and bluff. She'd see to it he lost every dollar he had. That
he lost it publicly, so that his humiliation would be complete.

"I want Sean O'Connell to lose as he never imagined,"
Alain had said in a whisper that chilled her to the bone. "To
lose everything, not just his money but his composure. His
pride. His arrogance. You are to leave him with only the
clothes on his back." He'd smiled then, a twist of the mouth
that had made her throat constrict. "And I'll give you a
bonus, darling. You can keep whatever you win. Won't that
be nice?"

Yes. Oh, yes, it would, because once she had that
money... Once she had it, she'd be free.

Until a little while ago, she hadn't let herself dwell on
that for fear Alain would somehow read her mind. Now, it
was all she could think about. She'd let Alain believe she
was doing this for him, but she was doing it for herself.

Herself and Missy.

When this night ended, she'd have the money she needed
to get away and to take care of her sister. They'd be free of
Alain, of what she'd finally realized he was... Of what she
feared he might want of her next.

If it took Sean O'Connell's humiliation, downfall and destruction to accomplish, so be it. She wouldn't, couldn't, concern herself about it. Why would she? O'Connell was a stranger.

He was also a thief.

He'd stolen a million dollars from Alain in a nonstop, three-day game of poker on Alain's yacht in the Mediterranean one year ago. She hadn't been there—it had been the first of the month and she'd been at the clinic in Geneva, visiting Missy—but Alain had filled her in on the details. How the game had started like any other, how he'd only realized O'Connell had cheated after the yacht docked at Cannes and O'Connell was gone.

Alain had spent an entire year plotting to get even.

The money wasn't the issue. What was a million dollars when you'd been born to billions? It was the principle of the thing, Alain said.

Savannah understood.

There were only three kinds of gamblers. The smart ones, the stupid ones and the cheats. The smart ones made the game exciting. Winning against someone as skilled as you was a dizzying high. The stupid ones could be fun, at first, but after a while there was no kick in taking their money.

The cheats were different. They were scum who made a mockery of talent. Cheat, get found out, and you got locked out of the casinos. Or got your hands broken, if you'd played with the wrong people.

Nobody called in the law.

Alain wanted to do something different. O'Connell had wounded him, but in a private setting. He would return the favor, but as publicly as possible. He'd finally come up with a scheme though he hadn't told her anything about his plan or the incident leading up to it until last week, right after she'd visited her sister.

He'd slipped his arm around her shoulders, told her what

had happened a year ago and what he wanted her to do. When she'd objected, he'd smiled that smile she'd never really noticed until a few months ago, the one that made her skin prickle.

"How's Missy?" he'd said softly. "Is she truly happy in that place, *chérie?* Is she making progress? Perhaps it's time for me to consider making some changes."

What had those words meant? Taken at face value they were benign, but something in his tone, his smile, his eyes gave a very different message. Savannah had stared at him, trying to figure out how to respond. After a few seconds, he'd laughed and pressed a kiss to her temple.

"It'll be fun for you, *chérie.* The coming-out party for your twenty-first birthday, so to speak."

What he meant was, she'd take O'Connell by surprise. She had yet to play in a casino; thus far, Alain had only let her sit in on private games.

She'd come to him at sixteen, straight off the streets of New Orleans where she'd kept herself and Missy alive scamming the tourists at games like three-card monte. She was good but her winnings were meager. You could only play for so long before the cops moved you on.

Alain had appeared one evening on the edge of the little crowd collected around her. He'd watched while she took some jerks who'd left their brains in their hotel rooms along with their baggage.

During a lull, he'd stepped in close.

"You're good, *chérie,*" he'd said with a little smile. He sounded French, but with a hint of New Orleans patois.

Savannah had looked him straight in the eye.

"The best," she'd said with the assurance of the streets.

Alain had smiled again and reached for her cards.

"Hey," she said, "leave those alone. They're mine."

He ignored her, moved the cards around, then stopped and looked at her. "Where's the queen?"

Savannah rolled her eyes and pointed. Alain grinned and moved the cards again. This time, his hands were a blur.

"Where is she now, *chérie?*"

Savannah gave him a piteous look and pointed again. Alain turned the card over.

No queen.

"Watch again," he said.

She watched again. And again. Five minutes later, she shook her head in amazement.

"How do you do that?"

He tossed down the cards and jerked his head toward the big black limo that had suddenly appeared at the curb.

"Come with me and I'll show you. You're good, *chérie,* but I'll teach you to use your mind as well as your hands. We can make a fortune together."

"Looks like you already got a fortune, mister."

That made Alain laugh. "I do, but there's always more. Besides, you intrigue me. You're dirty. Smelly."

"Hey!"

"But it's true, *chérie.* You look like an urchin and you sound like one, too, but there's a *je ne sais quoi* to you that intrigues me. You're a challenge. You'll be Eliza to my Professor Higgins."

"I don't know any Eliza or Professor Higgins," Savannah replied sourly.

"All you need to know is that I can change your life."

Did he take her for a fool? Four years in foster homes, one on the streets, and Savannah knew better than to get into a car with a stranger.

She also knew better than to let something good get away.

She'd looked at the limo, at the man, at his suit that undoubtedly cost more than she could hope to make in another five years of hustling. Then she looked at Missy, sitting placidly beside her on the pavement, humming a tune only she could hear.

Alain looked at Missy, too, as if he'd only just noticed her.

"Who is that?"

"My sister," Savannah replied, chin elevated, eyes glinting with defiance.

"What's wrong with her?"

"She's autistic."

"Meaning?"

"Meaning she can't talk."

"Can't or won't?"

It seemed a fine distinction no social worker had ever made.

"I don't know," Savannah admitted. "She just doesn't."

"There are doctors who can help her. *I* can help her. It's up to you."

Savannah had stared at him. Then she'd thought about the long, thin knife taped to the underside of her arm.

"You try anything funny," she'd said, her voice cold, her heart thumping with terror, "you'll regret it."

Alain had nodded and held out his hand. She'd ignored it, gently urged Missy to her feet and walked them both into a new life. Warm baths, clean clothes, nourishing food, a room all her own and a wonderful residential school for Missy.

And he had kept his word. He'd taught her everything he knew until she knew the odds of winning with any combination of cards in any game of poker, blackjack or *chemin de fer*.

He hadn't touched her, either.

Until recently.

Until he'd started looking at her through eyes that glit-

tered, that lingered on her body like an unwelcome caress
and made the hair rise on the back of her neck. Until he'd
taken to pressing moist kisses into the palm of her hand
and, worse still, calling her from her room in his chateau or
her cabin on his yacht whenever he had visitors, showing
her off to men whose eyes glittered as his did, who stroked
their fingers over her cheekbones, her shoulders.

Which was why she'd agreed to take Sean O'Connell to
the cleaners.

It was the best possible deal. Alain would get what he
wanted. So would she. By the night's end, she'd have
enough money to leave Alain and take care of Missy without his help. To run, if she had to—though surely she
wouldn't have to run from Alain.

He'd let her go.

Of course he would.

Savannah raised the champagne flute to her lips. It was
empty. Just as well. She never drank when she played. Tonight, though, she'd asked for the Cristal at the bar, felt the
need of its effervescence in her blood.

Not anymore.

She put her empty glass on a table and smoothed down
the shockingly short skirt of the red silk slip dress Alain
had selected. It wasn't her style, but then the life she was
living wasn't her style, either.

Savannah took a deep breath and emptied her mind of
everything but the game. She shook back her long golden
hair and stepped out of the shadows.

Ready or not, Sean O'Connell, here I come.

CHAPTER TWO

GOLDILOCKS was finally going to make her move.

Sean could sense it. Something in the way she lifted her glass to her mouth, in the way she suddenly seemed to draw herself up, gave her away. He wanted to applaud.

About time, babe, he felt like saying. *What took you so long?*

Of course, he didn't. Why give the game away now? He'd have bet a thousand bucks she had no idea he'd been watching her, no idea he was even aware of her.

He was.

He'd noticed her as soon as he'd entered the casino. Or not entered it, which, he supposed, was a better way of putting it. He'd learned, long ago, that it was better to take his time, scope a place out, get the feel of things instead of walking right into a situation. So he'd been taking his time, standing in the arched entry between the foyer and the high-stakes gaming room, sipping Jack Daniel's on the rocks as he watched.

Watched the tables. The players. The dealers. In a casino as in life, it paid to watch and wait.

That was when he'd noticed the blonde.

She was tall, with a great body and legs that went on forever. Her face might have inspired Botticelli and just the sight of that lion's mane of sun-streaked, silky-looking hair made him want to run his fingers through it.

Sean sipped his bourbon.

Oh, yeah. He'd noticed her, all right.

She was checking things out, too. At least, that was what he'd thought. After a while, he realized he had it wrong.

What she was checking out was him.

She was careful about it. Nothing clumsy or overt. She'd chosen her spot well. The lighting in the little alcove where she stood was dim, probably in deliberate contrast to the bright lights in the gaming area.

But Sean had long ago learned that the devil was in the details. The success of his game depended on it. He saw everything, and saw it without making people aware he was looking. One seemingly casual glance and he could figure out how Lady Luck was treating players just by taking in the expressions on their faces, or even the way they handled their cards.

Besides, a man would have to be blind not to have seen the blonde. She was spectacular.

And she was gearing up for something. Something that involved him. The only question was, what?

He'd thought about walking up to her, looking into those green eyes and saying, *Hello, sugar. Why are you watching me?*

It wasn't an opening line to use on a woman if she was about to come on to you, but instinct told him the blonde didn't have girl-meets-boy on her mind. No use pretending that wasn't unusual, Sean thought without a trace of ego. He was as lucky with women as he was with cards. That was just the way it was.

So, what was happening? Goldilocks was getting ready for something and it was making her nervous. He'd seen her hand tremble once or twice when she raised her champagne glass to her lips.

Curiosity had almost gotten the better of him when she began to move.

Sean narrowed his eyes as she stepped from the alcove and started toward him. Yes, the face was beautiful. Definitely Botticelli. But the body reminded him of a classical Greek sculpture. High, firm breasts. Slender waist. Those legs.

And a walk that made the most of all her assets.

Spine straight. Shoulders back. Arms swinging as she strutted toward him, crossing one long leg over the other so that she moved more like a tigress than a woman. It was a model's walk. He'd dated a German supermodel last year; Ursula had done The Walk for him in his living room, wearing nothing but a sultry pout and a lace teddy.

Goldilocks wasn't wearing a smile and her dress covered more than a teddy, though not much more. It was a scrap of crimson silk. He liked the way it clung to her breasts and hips. She had great hips, curved for the fit of a man's hands...

Hell.

He was getting hard just watching her.

Sean downed the last of his bourbon, told himself to concentrate on cold showers and on solving the puzzle of why the blonde had been observing him with such caution.

She was only a few feet away now. She hesitated. Then she lifted her chin, tossed back her hair, took a deep breath and smiled.

He felt the wattage straight down to his toes.

"Hi."

The tip of her tongue crept out, slicked across her bottom lip. Sean almost groaned but he managed a smile of his own.

"Hi yourself," he said. "I'd ask where you've been all my life, but you'd probably slug me for using such a trite line."

She laughed. And blushed. Another nice touch. He

couldn't recall the last time he'd seen a woman blush, but her smile still glittered.

"Not at all. Actually, I was wondering how to tell you I was here alone, and that I've been alone for too long."

Her voice was soft. A liquid purr. It reminded him of honey and warm Southern nights. He moved closer.

"Isn't it fortunate that I finally got here?" he said softly. "What's your name, sugar?"

"Savannah."

"Ah."

"Ah?"

"The name suits you. You have moonlight and magnolias in that sexy drawl. You're a Georgia girl."

Another rush of pink to her cheeks. Interesting, that she'd blush and still be so direct in coming on to him.

"Savannah what?"

She touched her tongue to her lips again. Did she know what that was doing to him? The tip of that pink tongue sweeping moistly across her rosebud mouth? He thought she did but when he looked into her eyes, he wasn't so sure. They were a clear green, but there seemed to be a darkness hidden in their depths.

"Just Savannah." She closed the little distance that remained between them. He could smell her scent, a seductively innocent blend of vanilla and woman. "No last names tonight. Is that okay?"

"It's fine." Sean cleared his throat. "I'm a sucker for a good mystery, Just-Savannah."

"Just…?" Her eyebrows rose. Then she smiled. "I like that. 'Just-Savannah.'"

"Good. That gives us two things in common. Honesty and anonymity. That's a fascinating combination, don't you think?"

"Yes. I do. What shall I call you?"

"Sean."

Something flickered in those incredible eyes. Relief? No. It couldn't have been that. Why would a simple exchange of names inspire relief?

"Just-Sean," she said, smiling.

"Just-Sean, and Just-Savannah. Two people without last names who meet and set out to discover what the rest of the night holds in store."

"I like that." She reached out and laid her hand lightly against his chest. "What game will you play tonight, Sean?"

He felt his body clench like a fist. "It depends on who I'm playing it with," he said hoarsely. "What did you have in mind?"

She laughed. Her teeth were small, even, very white against the golden tan of her skin.

"I'm not sure." Her eyes met his, then dropped away. "I'm new at this."

It was a great line, designed to set a man's hormones pumping. All of it was designed for that: the face, the body, the scrap of red silk and the sexy, let's-get-it-on banter...and yet, the only part of it he bought into was her being new at this. Somehow, that rang with truth.

The lady wasn't a pro.

Like moths to the proverbial flame, high-priced working girls were drawn to places where big money and big players congregated, but no matter how elegantly dressed and groomed they were, Sean could spot them at a hundred paces. Besides, a call girl would never get past the door of a private casino like L'Emeraude.

No, Savannah wasn't a pro. She had the looks and the lines, but her delivery was off. It was like listening to an actress who was still learning her part. And there were those moments he'd seen her hand tremble...as the one she'd put against his chest was doing now.

She was working at turning him on and she was succeeding, but she wasn't lying. She was, he was sure, a novice at this game. As flattering as it was to think she'd turned into a lust-crazed creature at the sight of him, he didn't buy it. There was the way she'd been watching him. Besides, he was too much of a realist to believe in bolts of lightning that struck with no warning.

Something else was going on here. He didn't know what, but he was damned well going to find out.

"Sean?"

He focused his gaze on the blonde's upturned face. The smile was still there but the pretty flush in her cheeks was back. Was she flustered? Embarrassed? Or was it part of the act?

"Sean. Have I been too... I mean, I'm sorry if—"

"Savannah." He smiled and covered her hand with his. Her skin was icy. Instinctively, he closed his fingers around hers. "A beautiful woman should never apologize for anything." Sean raised her hand to his mouth and pressed his lips to her knuckles. "Let's make a pact."

"A pact?"

"You won't say you're sorry again, and I'll buy you a glass of champagne. Okay?"

She took a long time before she answered. Then, just when he'd decided she was going to turn him down, she nodded.

"That would be lovely."

"Good." Sean's hand tightened on hers. "You have any thoughts on how to seal our agreement?"

Another rush of color swept into her face. "What do you mean?"

"It's simple. We have a contract." Sean lowered his

voice to a husky whisper. "Now we need some way to guarantee it." He looked at her slightly parted lips, then into her eyes. "You know. Sign in blood. Swear before witnesses. Cross your heart and hope to die." He flashed a quick smile. "Something to make it official."

He watched her face, saw the exact second she decided she'd had enough. Or maybe she'd decided to change tack. Try as he might, he couldn't tell which.

"You're making fun of me," she said.

"No, I'm not."

"You are. You think this is funny, and you're teasing me."

"Teasing. Not making fun. There's a world of difference."

"Let go of my hand, please."

"Why? I turn you on. You turn me on. That hasn't changed. Why walk away from it before we've discovered what comes next?"

He didn't know what he'd expected, though he'd gone out of his way to provoke a reaction. Would she blush some more? Lean into him and lift that luscious mouth to his? The combination of brashness and modesty was charming, even exciting, but it only made him more suspicious.

Whatever he might have anticipated, it wasn't the way she suddenly stood straighter, or the way her chin lifted.

"You're right," she said. "Why walk away now?"

Sean nodded. "That's better." It wasn't. She sounded as if she'd decided to go to the dentist after all. What in hell was happening? Acting on impulse, he reached out, put his hand under her chin and tilted her face up. "As for that contract," he said softly, "I know exactly how to seal the deal."

All of her was trembling now, not just the hand pressed to his chest. For a woman who'd tried to convince him of how eager she was to jump his bones, the lady was strangely nervous.

Sean smiled into her eyes, deliberately dropped his gaze to her mouth.

"No," she said quickly, the word a breathless whisper. "Please, don't—"

He hadn't intended to go through with it. The idea was to see how she'd react to the prospect of a kiss but when he saw her lips part, her eyes turn into the fresh green of a meadow after a spring rain, a shudder ran through his body. He wanted to kiss her. Kiss her, take her in his arms, carry her out of the noise and the light to a place where they'd be alone, where he could kiss her again and again until she trembled, yes, but trembled with need for him.

Sean stepped back, his pulse hammering, every muscle in his body tight as steel.

"Don't toast a deal with a bottle of champagne?" he said with forced lightness. "Now, that's definitely something no woman's ever asked of me before."

"Champ..." She caught her bottom lip between her teeth. He tried not to imagine it was his lip those perfect teeth were worrying. "Oh. I didn't... I mean, that would be nice."

"Besides, how could I let you go until I know why you stood in that alcove watching me for so long?"

Her face whitened. "I was not watching you."

"Telling fibs isn't nice, sugar. Sure you were. And now you're as nervous as a cat in a dog pound. Don't get me wrong, sweetheart. I like getting beautiful women flustered—but I like to know the reason for it. Somehow, I don't think your nerves have all that much to do with my masculine charms."

She looked up at him, conflicting emotions warring in her eyes. For a heartbeat, Sean felt as if she were on the verge of telling him something that would set him on a white charger like a knight ready to do battle with a dragon.

But she only smiled and angled her chin so she was gazing up at him through thick, honey-brown lashes.

"You're right about my watching you," she said softly, "but wrong in thinking it had nothing to do with your masculine charms." She smiled again, just enough to give those words the light touch they deserved. "I hoped you wouldn't notice."

"There's not a man in the room wouldn't notice you, if you were looking at him."

She laughed. It was a flirty, delicious sound. "That's very sweet."

"It's the truth."

Her hand was on his chest again, her fingers toying lightly with the lapel of his jacket. Her lips were slightly parted; she tilted her head back and now he could see the swift beat of her pulse in the hollow of her throat.

Sean almost groaned. He'd played games like this before but he'd never felt as if every muscle in his body was on full alert until now.

"I think it's time we got to know each other better, Just-Savannah."

"That sounds nice. What do you have in mind?"

Taking her to bed. That was what he had in mind, but he wasn't going to do that until he knew exactly what was going on here.

"The champagne I promised you, for starters." He linked his fingers through hers. "And some privacy."

"I'd like that."

Warning bells rang in his head. The words were right. So was the come-and-get-me smile, but the look in her eyes was wrong.

Maybe it was time to up the ante.

He turned her hand palm-up and lifted it to his mouth. He felt her stiffen as he pressed his lips to her flesh, felt her start to jerk her hand from his.

"Easy, sugar. I haven't taken a bite out of a woman in years. Not unless she wanted me to."

"I know. I just—I told you, this is all—"

"—new. Yeah, so you said." Sean's smile was deliberately lazy. "Unless, of course, there's more to the story than you're letting on."

"What more could there be, Mr. O'Connell? You're a very attractive man. I'm sure I'm not the first woman to show an interest in you."

The warning bells were going crazy. Mr. O'Connell? How could she know his name? He was Just-Sean. She was Just-Savannah. Definitely, there was more on her agenda. Should he call her on it? Should he play along?

He looked deep into the green eyes fixed to his. Hell. He was a gambler, wasn't he? What did he have to lose?

"Now, sugar," he said softly, "what kind of gentleman would I be if I answered that question?"

A slow, easy smile curved his mouth.

Seeing it, Savannah almost sagged with relief. For one awful minute, she'd been afraid she'd given everything away. She'd come awfully close, saying the wrong things, letting her nerves show, but then she'd turned the situation around by using her mistakes to convince Sean O'Connell she'd never come on to a man before.

That, at least, was the truth.

She couldn't afford any more screw-ups.

She'd thought this would be easy, but it wasn't. Using a deck of cards to scam a dumb mark on a dingy street corner was not the same as using your body, your smile, your words to scam an intelligent man in an elegant casino.

Besides, O'Connell was more than intelligent. He was

street-smart. She hadn't expected that. He kept looking at her as if she were a candy bar he wanted to unwrap, but always with a wariness that made her uneasy.

Not that it changed anything.

She was in too far to stop. Either she went forward or she failed. And failure wasn't an option.

He was still smiling, but was there something in his eyes that shouldn't be there? Time to come up with a clever move that would shut down his brain.

A squeeze of her fingers in his might do it. A sexy smile. A flick of her tongue across her bottom lip. He'd reacted to that before.

Yes. It was working. His eyes were darkening, focusing on her mouth.

"If you told me about those other women," she said huskily, "you'd be the kind of man I'd run from. I don't want you thinking about anyone but me tonight."

"There's no way I could," he said softly. Another light brush of his lips against her palm and then he tucked her hand into the crook of his arm. "Have you seen the terrace, Just-Savannah?"

"No." Her voice sounded thready. She cleared her throat. "No," she repeated, and smiled up at him, almost weak with relief. Things were back on track. "No, I haven't. I've never been here before."

"Then you're in for a treat." He began walking slowly through the casino. Because of the way he'd captured her hand, she was pressed close to his side, aware of the warm length of his body, aware of the muscles in his thigh as it shifted against hers. "Let's have a drink on the terrace and I'll show you the most beautiful sight in these islands." He glanced at her, angled his head down to hers and put his lips to her ear. "I take that back, sugar. The second most beautiful sight in these islands."

The warmth of his breath, the promise in his words sent a tingle of anticipation through her. For a moment, Savannah let herself imagine what it would be like if the story she'd spun were true. If she'd come here to gamble, noticed this tall, incredibly good-looking stranger, taken her courage in her hands and gone up to him with seduction, real seduction, in mind.

But she hadn't. She was here for a purpose.

Was O'Connell really as good a poker player as people claimed? Alain said he was.

Maybe. But she was better.

Tonight, that was all that mattered.

CHAPTER THREE

SEAN PAUSED just before they reached the terrace and signaled for a waiter, who hurried to his side.

"Sir?"

Sean drew Savannah a little closer. "What were you drinking, sugar? Cristal?"

She smiled. "Good guess."

"A bottle of Cristal Brut," Sean told the waiter. "Nineteen ninety. Will that be all right, Savannah?"

"It'll be lovely."

The waiter acknowledged the order with a discreet bow, and Sean opened the double glass doors that led onto the terrace.

"Here you are, sweetheart. The most beautiful night sky of the season, for the most beautiful woman in the Bahamas."

He put his hand lightly in the small of her back as they walked to the edge of the terrace. Her dress plunged in a deep vee to the base of her spine and her bare skin was as warm and silky as the tropical breeze drifting in from the sea.

"Oh," she said in a delicate whisper. "Oh, yes. It's perfect!"

"Perfect," he murmured, his eyes not on the softly illuminated pink sand beach or the star-shot black sky, but on her.

"It's so quiet."

"Yeah." A breeze lifted a strand of her golden hair and blew it across her lips. He caught it in his fingers and tucked it behind her ear, letting his touch linger. "Quiet, dark and private."

Did she stiffen under his caress? No, it was his imagination. He was sure of it when she looked at him, her lips upturned in a Mona Lisa smile.

"Quiet, dark and private," she said softly. "I like that."

He felt his body stir. "Me, too," he whispered, and bent his head to hers.

Her mouth was sweet and soft. One taste, and he knew it wouldn't be enough to satisfy the hunger building inside him. Sean swept his fingers into Savannah's hair and lifted her face to his.

He sensed this could be dangerous. She wanted something from him and he still didn't know what it was, but kissing her was irresistible. Even as he let himself sink into the kiss, he told himself it was okay, that playing along was the only way to find out what she was up to.

It was a great plan...except, he had miscalculated. He couldn't think, couldn't find out anything when deepening the kiss almost drove him to his knees.

God, her mouth! Soft. Honeyed. Hot. And the feel of her hair, sliding like silk over his fingers. The sigh of her breath as it mingled with his.

Sean forgot everything but the woman pressed against him.

"Savannah," he murmured, sliding his hands down her throat, her shoulders, lifting her to him, drawing her tightly into his arms.

She made a little sound. A whisper of surrender. Her lips softened. Parted. She was trembling, as if the world were shifting under her feet just as it was under his, and he gathered her against his body until her softness cradled the swift urgency of his erection.

She stirred in his arms, moved against him, and the blood pounded through his veins. Groaning, he moved his hand over her thigh, swept it under that sexy excuse of a skirt…

Just that quickly, she went crazy. Gasped against his mouth. Writhed in his arms. Twisted against him.

Sean thought she'd gone over the edge with desire. Thought it, right until she sank her teeth into his bottom lip.

"Goddammit," he yelped, and thrust her from him.

Stunned, tasting his own blood, he grabbed his handkerchief from his pocket and held it to his lip. The snowy-white linen square came away smeared with crimson. He stared at Savannah, his testosterone-fogged brain struggling for sanity. Her eyes were wide and glittering, her face drained of color, and he realized, with dawning amazement, that she hadn't moaned in surrender but in desperation.

She hadn't been struggling to get closer but to get away.

"Oh God," she whispered. She took a step toward him, hands raised in supplication. "I'm sorry."

"What the hell kind of game are you playing, lady?"

"No game. I didn't—I didn't mean to—to—"

Her hair was wild, the golden strands tumbling over her breasts. Her mouth was pink and swollen from his. Even now, knowing she was crazy, he couldn't help thinking how beautiful she was—and how crazy *he'd* be, if he spent a minute more in her company.

"Sean. I really am terribly sorry."

"Yeah. Me, too." He held the handkerchief to his lip again. The wound was starting to throb. "It's been interesting," he said, brushing past her. "I just hope the next guy you zero in on has better luck."

"Sean!" Her voice rose as she called after him. "Please. If you'd just give me a minute…"

He kept walking, but he was tempted. The bite hadn't been passion but what? Anger? Fear? He didn't know and told himself he didn't care. He wasn't a social worker. Whatever this woman's problem was, he wasn't the solution.

But she'd felt so soft. So vulnerable. When he'd first kissed her, she'd responded. It wasn't until he'd put his hand under her skirt that she'd panicked, if that was what she'd done, and that didn't make a whole lot of sense, not when she'd been damned near asking him to screw her for the past hour.

"Mr. O'Connell! Please!"

He stopped and swung around. She was running toward him. Mr. O'Connell, huh? Sean narrowed his eyes. Two times now, she'd called him that. Pretty surprising, since they hadn't introduced themselves with last names.

So much for walking away.

Why had she pretended not to know who he was? Why act as if she wanted to sleep with him when she'd gone from soft sweetness to what sure as hell seemed to be terror at the touch of his hand?

She stopped a few feet away.

"Please," she said again, her voice a shaky whisper. "I didn't meant to—to—" She swallowed dryly. "Your lip is still bleeding."

"Yeah?" He forced a thin smile. "What a surprise."

She closed the distance between them, that elegant feline walk gone so that she wobbled a little on her sky-high, dome-baby heels.

"Let me fix it."

"Thanks, but you've done enough already."

She wasn't listening. Instead, she was burrowing inside her ridiculously small evening purse. What'd she expect to find? he thought grimly. A bottle of antiseptic and a cotton swab?

"Here. Just duck your head a little."

A froth of white lace. That was what she pulled from the purse. Sean glowered at her. She stared back. He could see her confidence returning, the glitter of defiance starting to replace the fear in her eyes.

"I'm not going to hurt you, Mr. O'Connell."

A muscle jerked in his jaw. "That's what they all say."

That brought a twitch to her lips. Sean told himself he was an idiot, and did as she'd asked.

Gently, she patted the handkerchief against the wound she'd inflicted, concentrating as if she were performing open-heart surgery. The pink tip of her tongue flicked out and danced along the seam of her mouth, and Sean felt his traitorous body snap to attention.

"There," she said briskly. "That should do—"

He hissed with pain as she pulled the hankie away. A bit of lace had clung to the congealing blood; yanking it free had started a tiny scarlet trickle oozing.

Savannah raised stricken eyes to his.

He'd gotten it right the first time. Her eyes really were as green as a spring meadow. And her mouth was pink. Like cotton candy. Maybe that wasn't very poetic, but he'd always loved the taste of cotton candy.

"I'm sorry," she said on a note of despair. "I know I keep saying that but—"

"You have to moisten it." His voice rumbled and he cleared his throat. "The handkerchief. If it's damp, it won' stick to the cut."

"Oh." She looked around. "You're right. Just give me a minute to find the ladies'—"

"Wet it with your tongue," he said. Hell. Now he sounded as if he'd run his words through a bed of gravel

Her eyes rose to his again. "The hankie. You know. Just—just use your mouth to make it wet."

Her face turned the same color as her dress. Time stretched between them, taut as a wire.

"Sean," she said quietly, "I didn't— When you kissed me, I didn't expect—I didn't know—"

"Know what?" he said roughly, moving closer. He reached out, cupped her face.

"Sir?"

Sean swung around. The waiter stood a few feet away.

"Your champagne, sir. Shall I...?"

"Just—" Sean cleared his throat. "Just put it on that table. No, don't open it. I'll do it myself."

Saved by the proverbial bell, he thought as the waiter did as he'd asked. Kissing this woman again made about as much sense as raising the ante with a pair of threes in your hand.

He waited until they were alone again, taking the time to get himself back under control. Then he looked at Savannah.

"Champagne," he said briskly.

"For what?" She'd pulled herself together, too. Her voice was strong, her color normal.

"It's just what we need. For the cut on my lip."

"Oh. Oh, of course. Will you—"

"Sure."

Sean did the honors, twisting the wire muzzle from the neck of the bottle, then popping the cork. The wine sparkled with bubbles as he poured some on the hankie she held out.

"It'll probably sting," she said, and before he could reply, she moved in and dabbed the cut with the cold, wine-soaked lace.

An understatement, Savannah thought, as Sean O'Connell rocked back on his heels.

"Sorry," she said politely. The hell she was, she thought.

She'd made a damned fool of herself. Worse, she'd probably blown her chance at setting him up for the kill, but it was his fault.

Why did he have to ruin things by kissing her? If he hadn't, everything would still be fine. She hadn't meant for him to kiss her; she was supposed to be the one setting the boundaries for this little escapade, not him.

"Hey! Take it easy with that stuff."

"Sorry," she said again, and went right on cleaning the cut with as little delicacy as she could manage.

Some seductress she was. The mark made a move she hadn't anticipated, gave her one simple kiss, and…

Except, it hadn't been a simple kiss. It had been as complex as the night sky. She'd trembled under it. The texture of his mouth. The whisper of his breath. The silken glide of his tongue against hers.

And then—then, it had all changed. His hand on her thigh. The quick bloom of heat between her legs. The pressure of his hard, aroused male flesh, the message implicit in its power.

All at once, the terrace had become the yacht. She'd remembered the way Alain's friends had taken to looking at her and the way Alain talked to them right in front of her, his voice pitched so low she couldn't hear his words.

She didn't have to.

She had only to see their hot eyes, see the little smiles they exchanged, feel the way a beefy hand would brush against her breast, her thigh, always accidentally…

"Are you trying to fillet my lip or leave it steak *tartare?*"

Savannah blinked. O'Connell, arms folded over his chest, was eyeing her narrowly, his face expressionless.

"I, uh, I just wanted to make sure I disinfected the cut properly." She dropped her hand to her side, peered at his lip as if she knew what she was doing and flashed what she hoped was a brilliant smile. "It looks fine."

"Does it," he said coldly.

Oh, this wasn't any good! She'd had him right where she wanted him, and now she'd lost him. He was furious and she couldn't blame him.

Well, that would have to change if she was going to get anywhere tonight.

"Yes," she said, with a little smile. "I'm happy to tell you, you won't need stitches. No rabies shots, either."

He didn't smile back. All right. One more try.

"I suppose I owe you an apology," she said, looking at him from under her lashes.

Sean almost laughed. The cute smile. The tease. And, when those failed, the demure look coupled with an apology. All designed to tap into his masculine instincts. He was supposed to say "no, it's okay," because that was what a gentleman would do.

Unfortunately for Just-Savannah, he was no gentleman.

"No."

"No?"

"I don't want an apology."

She almost sighed with relief. He waited a beat.

"I want an explanation."

She blinked. Clearly, she hadn't expected that. Now she was mentally scrambling for a response.

"An explanation," she parroted. "And—and you're entitled to one. I, uh, I think it's just that you—you caught me by surprise."

"You've been coming on to me all evening."

"Well—well, I told you, you're an attractive—"

She gasped as he caught hold of her wrists.

"And yet, the first move I make, you react as if I dragged you into an alley."

"That's not—"

"Game's over, sweetheart."

"I have no idea what you're talking about."

"Nobody plays me for a fool." Sean held her tighter, applying just enough pressure to let her know he was taking charge. "I want answers."

"To what? Honestly, Mr. O'Connell…"

"Let's start with the 'Mr. O'Connell' routine. I was Just-Sean. You were Just-Savannah. How come it turns out you know my last name?"

Savannah swallowed past the lump in her throat. His face was like a thundercloud; his hands were locked around hers like manacles. *Missy,* she thought, *oh, Missy, I'm so sorry.*

"I told you," she said in a low voice. "I saw you and I found you very—"

"Forget that crap." His mouth thinned; he tugged on her wrists and she had no choice but to stumble forward until they were only a breath apart. "I knew something was up, but you were determined to keep trying the same con so I decided to go along. You've been scamming me, sugar, and I've had enough. You tell me what's going on or I'll drag you to the manager's office and see to it you're barred from ever entering this place again."

"You can't do that! I have as much right to be here as you do."

"Maybe you're a working girl."

"A working…" She began to tremble. "That's a lie."

"Is it? Once I describe your behavior, who's going to argue with me?"

"You can't do that!"

His grin was all teeth. "Try me."

Savannah opened her mouth, then shut it. For all she knew, he could do anything. He was known here. She wasn't. Everything was coming apart. She'd have to go back to Alain and tell him she'd failed, that his year of planning had led to nothing.

"Well? I'm waiting for that explanation. And I'll tell you right now, sugar, it damned well better be good."

Desperate, she searched for anything that might get her out of this mess. What could she possibly say that would change things? O'Connell was right. He wasn't about to believe she was interested in him, not after she'd almost bitten his face off when he touched her.

She wouldn't react that way if he did it again.

The realization shocked her. It was true, though. Now that she knew what to expect, if it happened again—which it wouldn't—but if it did, if she ever felt all that heat, saw the hunger in his eyes, she might just—she might just—

"Okay, that's it."

Sean started walking toward the door, dragging her with him. *Think,* she told herself desperately, *think, think!*

"All right," she gasped. "I'll tell you the truth."

He swung toward her, towering over her in the moonlight. He said nothing. Clearly, the next move was hers. Savannah took a steadying breath and played for time to work out a story. Something he would buy so she wouldn't have to return to Alain in failure and see that cool smile, hear him say, *Ah, chérie, that's too bad. I hate to think of your dear little sister in one of those state institutions.*

She took a steadying breath. "I owe you an apology, Mr. O'Connell."

"You already said that."

"Not for biting you. For—what did you call it? For scamming you."

It was a start. At least she'd caught his attention.

"I didn't mean to. Not exactly. I just—"

"You didn't mean to. Not exactly." Sean raised an eyebrow. "That's your explanation?"

"No! There's more."

"Damned right, there's more. Why don't you start by telling me why you pretended not to know who I was?"

How much of the truth could she tell, without giving everything away?

"I'm waiting."

"Yes. I know." She looked down at their hands, still joined, then up at his face. "It's true. I did know who you were. Well, I knew your name but then, everyone knows your name."

She fell silent. Sean let go- of her wrists and tucked his hands into his pockets. He'd long ago learned the art of keeping quiet. Do it right and the other person felt compelled to babble.

"Everyone knows you're the world's best poker player."

He wasn't, though he was close to it. Still, he said nothing. She didn't, either, but he knew his silence was getting to her. She was chewing lightly on her lip. If she wasn't careful, she'd leave a little wound to match his.

A wound he could easily soothe with a flick of his tongue. *Damn, where had that thought come from?*

"And all this is leading where?" he said gruffly.

"To—to the reason I came over and spoke to you."

"Sugar," he said, smiling tightly, "you didn't speak to me, you hit on me. Understand, I've no objection to a beautiful woman showing her interest." His smile faded. "I just don't like being played for a sucker."

"I didn't—"

"Yeah, you did. Or you would have, if you could have gotten away with it." He pulled his hand from his pocket and checked his watch. "I have other things to do tonight. You have two minutes to answer my questions—or we can take that walk to the office."

Savannah knotted her fingers together. She was going to

do the very thing Alain had warned her against, but what other choice did she have?

"I play poker, too, Sean."

"How nice." His teeth showed in a chilly smile. "We're back to first names."

"Did you hear what I—"

"You said you play poker. What's that got to do with anything?"

She hesitated. What could she safely tell him? Surely not that the man he'd cheated out of a million dollars had sent her, or that she was going to wipe him out because she was as good a player as he'd ever met.

She certainly couldn't tell him the rest of it, that she'd planned to work him into such a sexual haze that by the time they sat down to play, he'd be so busy drooling over her that he wouldn't be able to concentrate on his cards.

But she could tell him part of it, fancy things up to appeal to his ego. She'd blown her cover as a *femme fatale*. Could she pass herself off as an overeager tourist?

"I'm American. Like you."

"Congratulations," Sean said dryly. "So what?"

"So, I'm on vacation. You know. Sun, sea, sand. Gambling. I really like to gamble, even though I'm new at it."

A muscle flickered in his jaw. "Go on."

"You're right about my name. I was born in Georgia but I live in Louisiana. That's where I learned to play cards. On a riverboat. You know, on the Mississippi? A date took me, the first time." She grinned, hoped it was disarming and that mixing lies and truth proved the ticket to success. "I picked up the game fast. I'm pretty good, if I must say so myself, but I've never played against serious competition. Against, say, a man like you."

Sean lifted an eyebrow. Was this the whole thing? Had she flirted with him just to convince him to take a seat at the same poker table? Anything was possible. Novices approached him all the time. In his own tight little world, he was a celebrity of sorts.

Except, he didn't buy it.

All this subterfuge, so he could beat her pretty tail off in a game of cards? So she could go home and say she'd played Sean O'Connell?

No way.

"I'd be thrilled if you'd let me sit at a table with you, Sean. I could go home and tell everyone—"

"Anybody can sit at any table. You must know that."

"Well—well, of course I know that. But I'm not that forward. I know you think I am, after all that's happened, but the truth is, I wouldn't have the courage to take a seat at a table you were at unless I cleared it with you first."

He still didn't buy it. She wouldn't have the courage? This woman who'd done everything but jump his bones?

"And that's it?"

Savannah nodded. "That's it."

He moved fast, closed the distance between them before she could even draw a breath. All at once, her back was to the wall and his hands were flattened against it on either side of her.

"You took a big risk, sugar," he said softly. "Coming on to me as hard as you did without knowing a damned thing about me except that I play cards. You got me going a few minutes ago. If your luck had gone bad, you might have gotten hurt."

He saw her throat constrict as she swallowed, but her eyes stayed right on his.

"I told you that I knew you were Sean O'Connell. And Sean O'Connell isn't known for hurting women."

"No." His gaze fell to her mouth. He looked up and smiled. "He's known for liking them, though."

"Sean. About what I've asked…"

"Why did you panic?"

"I didn't. I—"

Sean put one finger gently over her lips. "Yeah, you did. I kissed you, you kissed me back, and then you got scared." His finger slid across the fullness of her mouth. "How come? What frightened you?"

"Nothing frightened me."

She was lying. He could sense it. There was something going on he still didn't understand and, all at once, he wanted to.

"Savannah." Sean cupped her face. "What's the matter? Tell me what it is. Let me help you."

Her eyes glittered. Was it because of the moonlight, or were those tears?

"I don't know what you're talking about."

Sean smoothed back her hair. "Just as long as you're not afraid of me," he said gruffly, and kissed her.

She let it happen, let herself drown in the heat of his kiss. She told herself it was what she had to do but when he drew back, she had to grasp his shoulders for support.

"Tell me what you want," he said softly.

Savannah willed her heart to stop racing. Then she took a deep breath and said the only thing she could.

"I told you. I want to play cards. Then I can go home and tell everybody that I played against the great Sean O'Connell."

"And that's it? That's all you need from me?"

His eyes were steady on hers, his body strong under her hands. For one endless moment, she thought of telling him the truth. That she was here to destroy him. That she was in trouble and had no one to turn to for help but herself.

Then she remembered that he was a thief, and she forced a smile to her lips.

"That's it," she said lightly. "That's all I need."

CHAPTER FOUR

Two HOURS LATER, Sean was sitting across from Savannah at a poker table in the high-stakes area of the casino and the warning bells in his head were clamoring like bells inside a firehouse.

The game was draw poker. She was still playing. He'd already folded, just as he'd done half a dozen times since they'd started. His fault, he knew. He'd played with lazy disinterest, underestimated the lady's skill.

And her skill was considerable.

The realization had caught him by surprise. Once it had, he'd played a couple of hands as he should have from the start. She'd folded. He'd won.

That had led to another realization. Goldilocks wasn't a good loser.

Oh, she said all the right things, the clever patter card-players used to defuse tension. She flashed that megawatt smile across the table straight at him. But her eyes didn't smile. They were dark with distress. What she'd said about simply wanting to play him wasn't true.

Just-Savannah needed to win. He decided to let her. There were all kinds of ways to up the ante.

And if she was new to the game, he was Mighty Mouse.

She played with the cool concentration of someone who'd had years to hone her talent. Her instincts were good, her judgment sharp, and by now he'd determined that the cute little things she did when she played, things he'd at first thought were unconscious habits, were deliberate shticks meant to distract him.

A little tug at a curl as it kissed the curve of her cheek. A brush of her tongue across her mouth. A winsome smile accompanied by a look from under the thick sweep of her gold-tipped lashes.

Most effective of all, a sigh that lifted her breasts.

The air-conditioned chill in the casino was cooperating. Each time her breasts rose, the nipples pressed like pearls against the red silk that covered them.

Forget about the odds, she all but purred. *Forget about the game. Just think about me. What I have to offer, you'll never get by winning this silly game of cards.*

It was hard not to do exactly that. The man in him wanted what she was selling with every beat of his heart. The gambler in him knew it was all a lie. And there it was again. The smile, just oozing with little-girl amazement that she was actually winning.

Bull.

Savannah wasn't a novice, she was an expert. Playing without using any of those distractions, she'd beat every man at the table on ability alone.

Every man but him.

She was good, but he was better. And once he knew what in hell was happening, he'd prove it to her.

Meanwhile, the action was fascinating to watch. Not just her moves but the moves of the rest of the players. Two— a German industrialist and a Texas oil billionaire—were good. The others—a prince from some godforsaken principality, a Spanish banker, a has-been American movie star and an Italian who had something to do with designing shoes—weren't. It didn't matter. The men were all happy to be losing.

Sean didn't think Savannah gave a damn. He'd have bet

everything he owned that she was putting on this little show solely for him.

Why? No way was it so she could go home and boast about having played against him. That story leaked like a sieve, especially because he could see past the smile, the cleavage, the performance art.

Under all that clever artifice, she was playing with a determination so grim it chilled him straight down to the marrow of his bones.

So he'd decided to lay back. Win a couple of hands, lose a couple. Fold early. Look as if he was as taken in as the others while he tried to figure out what was going on.

Right now, he and she were the only ones playing. The rest had all folded. She sighed. Her cleavage rose. She licked her lips. She twirled a curl of golden hair around her index finger. Then she looked at him and fluttered her lashes.

"I'll see your five," she said, "and raise you ten."

Sean smiled back at her. He didn't bother looking at his cards. He knew what he had and he was damned sure it beat what she was holding.

"Too rich for my blood," he said lazily, and dropped his cards on the green baize tabletop.

The German smiled. "The *fräulein* wins again."

Savannah gathered in the chips. "Beginner's luck," she said demurely, and smiled at him again.

It wasn't luck, beginner's or otherwise. The luck of the draw was a big part of winning but from what he'd observed, it had little to do with her success at this table.

The lady was good.

He watched as she picked up her cards, fanned them just enough to check the upper right-hand corners, then put them down again. It was a pro's trick. When your old man owned one of the biggest hotels and casinos in Vegas, you learned their tricks early.

Not that Sean had spent much time in the casino. State law prohibited minors from being in the gaming areas. More importantly, so did his mother.

One gambler in the family was enough for Mary Elizabeth O'Connell. She'd never complained about her husband's love of cards, dice, the wheel, whatever a man could lay a wager on, but she also made it clear she didn't want to see her children develop any such interests.

Still, Sean had been drawn to the life as surely as ocean waves are drawn to the shore.

He began gambling when he was in his teens. By his senior year in high school, he bet on anything and everything. Basketball. Football. Baseball. A friend's grades. His pals thought he was lucky. Sean knew better. It was more than luck. He had a feel for mathematics, especially for those parts of it that dealt in probability, combinations and permutations. Show him the grade spread for, say, Mrs. Keany's classes in Trig over the past five years, he could predict how the current grades would play out with startling accuracy.

It was fun.

Then he went away to college, discovered poker and fell in love with it. He loved everything about the game. The cool, smooth feel of a new deck of cards. The numbers that danced in his head as he figured out who was holding what. The kick of playing a hand he knew he couldn't lose or, conversely, playing a hand no sane man would hold on to and winning anyway because he was good and because, in the final analysis, even the risk of losing could give you an adrenaline rush.

By the time he graduated from Harvard with a degree in business, he had a small fortune stashed in the bank.

Sean handed his degree to Mary Elizabeth, kissed her on both cheeks and said he knew he was disappointing her but he wasn't going to need that degree for a while.

"Just don't disappoint yourself," she'd told him, her smile as gentle as her voice.

He never had.

After almost eight years playing in the best casinos and private games all around the world, he was one hell of a player. His bank account reflected that fact. He could risk thousands of dollars on each turn of the cards without blinking.

He didn't win all the time. That would have been impossible, but that was still part of what he loved about the game. The danger. The sense that you were standing on top of the world and only you could keep you there. It was part of the lure. Maybe it was all of it.

Maybe he just liked living on the edge.

He wasn't addicted to cards.

He was addicted to excitement.

And what was happening tonight, at *L'Emeraude de Caribe,* was as exciting as anything he'd experienced in a very long time.

A blonde with the face of a Madonna and the body of a courtesan was running a scam with him as the prospective patsy, and he was going to find out what she was up to or—

"O'Connell? You in or out?"

Sean looked up. The Texan grinned at him from around the dead cigar stub clamped in his teeth.

"I know the little lady's somethin' of a distraction," the Texan said in a stage whisper, "but you got to make a decision, boy."

"I'm in," Sean said, shoving a stack of chips to the center of the table.

Everyone was in, except for the prince. He dumped his

cards, folded his arms and never took his eyes from Savannah. She was, as the Texan had said, something of a distraction.

Soon, only he, Savannah and the German remained. The German folded. He had nothing. Sean had a pair of aces and two jacks. Could Savannah top that? He knew she couldn't. He raised her ten thousand. She saw it, smiled and raised another ten.

Should he meet it? Or should he let her think she'd out-bluffed him, the way he'd done the last few hands?

Savannah began her little act. The tongue slicking across her mouth. The breasts straining against the red silk.

He wondered how she'd look stripped of that silk. Her breasts seemed rounded, small enough to cup in his hands. Were her nipples as pink as her lips? Or were they the color of apricots? They'd taste like honey, he was certain. Wild-flower honey, and when he sucked them into his mouth, tugged at them with his teeth, her cry would fill the night...

"Mr. O'Connell?"

He blinked. Savannah was watching him intently, almost as if she knew what he was thinking.

"Are you in or out?"

He looked down at his cards again. The aces and the jacks looked back. What the hell, he thought.

"Out," he said, and dumped his cards on the table. He smiled at her. "You know, you're taking me to the cleaners, sugar."

It was true. He'd lost a lot of money. He wasn't sure how much. Seventy thousand. A hundred. More, maybe.

He waited for her to smile back at him. She didn't.

"You're not going to stop playing, are you? I mean—I mean, it's still early."

She sounded panicked. He'd had no intention of quitting. Now, he decided to pretend that he had.

"I don't know," he said lazily. "Heck, a man's a fool to keep playing when he's losing."

"Oh, come on." She smiled, but her lips barely moved. "One more hand."

Sean pretended to let her talk him into it. He watched her pick up the cards as the dealer skimmed them to her.

Her hands were trembling.

His cards were bad. Evidently, so were those of the others. Some fast mental calculations suggested Savannah's cards were excellent. The others dropped out. Sean raised the ante. Savannah folded before the words were fully out of his mouth.

"You won this time around," she said gaily, but he could hear the edge in her voice. And her hands were still shaking. "Aren't you glad you stayed in?"

Sean nodded and pulled the chips toward him. What she'd done didn't make sense. He was sure she'd had better than even odds on holding a winning hand. Had she folded only to make him want to stay in the game?

It was time to make a move. Change the momentum and see what happened.

"It's getting late," he said. He yawned, stretched, and pushed back his chair. "I think I've had it."

Savannah looked up. He could see her pulse beating in her throat.

"Had it? You mean you want to stop playing?"

"Enough is enough, don't you think?"

When she smiled, her lips damned near stuck to her teeth. "But you just won!"

"And about time, too," he said, and chuckled.

"Come on, O'Connell." The Texan flashed a good ol' boy grin. "You can't quit when the little lady's beatin' the pants off of all of us. Pardon me, ma'am, for bein' crude, but that's exactly what you're doin'."

"And we love it," the German said, chortling. "Come, come, Mr. O'Connell. Surely you won't walk away when things are just getting interesting. I don't think I've ever heard of you losing with such consistency."

"True," the prince said, and nudged the man with a sharp elbow, "but then, I doubt if Mr. O'Connell's accustomed to playing with such a charming diversion at the table."

Everyone laughed politely. Not Savannah. The expression on her face was intense.

"Please. I'd be devastated if you left now." Her voice was unsteady, but the smile she gave him was sheer enticement.

Sean decided to let her think it had worked. "Tell you what. How about we take a break? Fifteen minutes. Get some air, whatever. That okay with the rest of you?"

It was okay with everyone except Savannah, who looked as if he'd just announced he was abandoning ship, but she responded with a bright smile.

"That's fine," she said, pushing back her chair, too. "No need to get up," she added, when the men half rose to their feet. "I'll just—I'll just go to the powder room."

Sean watched her walk away. They all did, and it annoyed him. Stupid, he knew. He had no rights to her, nor did he want any. Still, he didn't like the way the others looked at her.

"She is a beautiful woman," the Italian said.

The one-time movie star smiled. "That she is."

"You're a lucky SOB, O'Connell," the Texan said, shifting the unlit cigar in his mouth.

Sean grinned. "Lucky to lose so much money?"

"Lucky to have a woman like that interested in you." The prince leaned forward. "I'd be happy to lose twice what I have, if she'd do that little tongue trick with me in mind."

Sean's smile vanished. "I'll be back," he growled, and headed for the terrace.

The terrace was as empty as when he'd been out there with Savannah. Empty, quiet, and a good place to get some fresh air and reconsider the point of letting a woman he didn't know think she was getting the best of him.

He walked to the rail, leaned against it and stared blindly out over the sea. Maybe he was dead wrong about Savannah. He could be reading things into the way she was behaving. Wasn't it possible she'd told him the truth? That all she wanted was to play cards? Those feminine tricks could just be part of the action. She might have used them to advantage back on the riverboat, where she said she'd learned to gamble.

And even if she was lying about being new to gambling, about wanting to play him...what did that change? Not a thing, he thought, answering his own question. He was making a mystery out of something that was probably, at best, simply an interesting situation.

If she was up to anything at all, it might just be scamming him so she could take him, big-time.

So what if he could still remember the sweet taste of her mouth? If her eyes were deep enough to get lost in?

If her hands trembled, and sometimes he saw a fleeting expression on her lovely face that made him want to gather her into his arms and kiss her, hold her, tell her he'd protect her from whatever it was she feared—

"Lovely night, Mr. O'Connell, isn't it?"

Sean started. The prince, who'd come up alongside him, inclined his head in apology.

"Sorry. I didn't mean to take you by surprise."

"That's okay. I was just—just listening to the sound of the sea. I didn't hear you coming."

The prince leaned back against the rail as he reached into

the pocket of his tuxedo jacket and took out a slim gold cigarette case. He opened it and held it out to Sean, who shook his head.

"No, thanks."

"You don't smoke?" Sighing, the prince put the cigarette in his mouth, flicked the wheel of a small gold lighter and put a flame to the tip. "I've been trying to quit for years." He exhaled a plume of smoke and smiled. "My wife assures me it's a worse affliction than gambling."

Sean nodded. He wasn't in the mood for conversation.

"And I assure her that a man must have some vices, or there isn't much point in living." The prince inhaled again. "She's a stunning young woman."

"I'm sure she is." Sean made a show of checking the luminous dial on his watch. "Would you excuse me, Prince Artois? I want to make a stop in—"

"I wasn't referring to my wife—though she is, of course, a beautiful woman." The prince blew out a perfect smoke ring. "I was talking about our poker player. Savannah."

Something in the man's tone made the hair rise on the back of Sean's neck.

"Yes," he said carefully, "she is."

"You're fortunate she has such an interest in you."

"She's interested in winning," Sean said, just as carefully. "We all are."

"And yet, you are losing. I doubt if anyone has ever seen you lose this way before."

"It happens."

"Indeed." The prince turned to stare out over the sea, the burning tip of his cigarette a tiny beacon in the night. "What I find most amusing is that she's so good that the rest of us would surely lose against her even if she weren't such a distraction, but you—you shouldn't be losing at all. You're not easily diverted, or so I've heard."

"Diverted?"

"Come on, O'Connell. You and I both know the lady is doing her best to keep your attention off the game."

"Perhaps she's succeeding," Sean said, his eyes fixed to the prince's autocratic profile.

"Perhaps. Or perhaps you're letting her win, for your own reasons."

Sean straightened up. "I'll see you inside."

He began walking toward the lighted door, but the prince called after him.

"You know who she is, of course?"

A muscle knotted in Sean's jaw. He stopped, but didn't turn around.

"A woman named Savannah," he said, "from the American South."

"Savannah McRae," Artois said. "That's her full name."

Slowly, Sean turned and looked at him. "You know her?"

"We've never been introduced until tonight." He gave Sean a thin smile. "But I know who she is. And what."

Sean went toward him, his steps deliberate, his eyes never leaving Artois's face.

"Would you like to explain that?"

"She plays cards." Artois flicked the glowing cigarette butt over the railing. It flickered like a tiny shooting star as it arced toward the beach. "It's how she earns her keep."

Her keep. Not her living, which would no longer have surprised Sean, but her keep.

"Her keep?" he asked softly.

"Is this really unknown to you, Mr. O'Connell?"

The muscle in Sean's jaw leaped. "Get to it, Artois," he growled, "and stop screwing around."

The prince smiled. "She's Alain Beaumont's mistress."

HE DIDN'T BELIEVE IT.

Savannah, Beaumont's mistress? No. It was impossible.

Sean paced the terrace on the other side of the casino, far from the sound of the surf, the lights, the all-too-vividly remembered taunting smile Artois had shown him.

Beaumont was slime. His little cruelties to the maids who worked in the elegant houses on these islands and in Europe were whispered about; his perversions were the topic of quiet speculation among those who found him either fascinating or revolting.

Sean had met him at a casino in Monte Carlo. Just watching him fondle the backside of a waitress whose face blazed with shame, hearing his lewd jokes, listening to his boasts about his sexual prowess, had been enough to make him despise Beaumont.

Somehow, they'd ended up playing at the same baccarat table, the same roulette wheel, the same poker table, where Beaumont lost to Sean. Lost badly.

Beaumont's eyes had burned with fury but his voice had been unctuous as he invited Sean to give him the chance to win back his money. Sean had wanted only to see the last of him, but honor meant accepting the challenge.

"Deal the cards," Sean had snapped.

But Beaumont refused. He wanted Sean to play on his yacht, anchored in the harbor. And because Sean wanted nothing more than to see the man lose again, he'd agreed.

They'd taken Beaumont's tender to the yacht, just the two of them, and played through the night and the morning, Beaumont's line of oily chatter gradually giving way to tight-lipped rage as the pile of chips in front of Sean grew.

By noon the next day, he'd won a million dollars. Beaumont slammed his hand on the table, called Sean a cheat. Sean grabbed him by his lapels, hauled him to his feet, demanded an apology or he'd beat him to a pulp.

He'd almost hoped Beaumont wouldn't oblige. Beating him insensible held enormous appeal.

But Beaumont conceded, making up for not giving Sean the chance to beat him by wetting his trousers. Sean had laughed in scorn, scooped up his money and left. Once on shore, he walked into the first charity office he found and gave his winnings to a shocked and delighted little old lady seated behind a battered desk.

He had not seen Beaumont since.

Sean reached the end of the terrace and came to a dead stop.

Savannah, Beaumont's mistress? That greasy pig, taking her into his bed? His thick lips sucking at hers? His hands on her breasts, his thigh parting hers, his...

Sean balled his hands into fists, threw his head back and glared up at the stars as if they were to blame for what had happened. God knew, the fault was his own. He'd been fooled by Alain Beaumont. Now, he'd been fooled by Beaumont's mistress.

Obviously, Savannah was supposed to win back the million Beaumont had lost.

Sean narrowed his eyes.

Beaumont wanted to play? Sean would oblige him, only this time, he'd lose more than his money.

He took a steadying breath, thrust his hands into his hair and smoothed it down. Then he strolled back into the casino.

Savannah was in her alcove again. Her back was to him; she had one hand to her ear. She was talking to someone on a cell phone.

Another deep breath, this time to keep himself from giving the game away. He approached her quietly, from behind.

"I understand," she was saying, her voice low-pitched. "Alain, yes, you've told me that already..."

Alain. Alain. Sean felt his stomach roil, again saw Savannah in the pig's arms.

"I will. Of course, I will. I just wanted you to know that it might not go as we'd— Because he's clever, that's why. There are moments I think he's on to me, and…" Her shoulders bowed. Her head drooped. "No," she whispered. "Alain, please, just give me a little more time."

Sean stared at Savannah's dejected posture. Heard the desperation in her voice. For one wild minute, he saw that white horse again, saw himself in silver armor, galloping toward her.

"Yes, Alain. You know I do. Do you need me to say it? You mean—you mean everything to me."

Sean's gut knotted. He thought about going to her, spinning her around, slapping her face even though he'd never laid a finger on a woman in his life.

Instead, he swallowed past the bitter taste in his throat.

"Savannah?" he said casually.

She spun around, her face turning white when she saw him.

"There you are," he said, and forced his lips to curve in a smile. "Where've you been, sugar? We said fifteen minutes, remember?"

She stared at him blankly. "Sean?"

He mounted the two steps that led into the alcove. "Who are you talking to, sugar?" Still smiling, he held out his hand. "The folks back home, I bet. Are you telling them how you're playing and winning?"

Slowly, she took the tiny phone from her ear and looked at it as if she'd never seen it before. Then she hit the button to end the call, opened her evening purse and dropped the phone inside.

"Yes," she said. Her smile was shaky but he had to give

her credit for managing to smile at all. "That's exactly what I was doing. They're all green with envy."

"I bet." Sean waggled his hand. She took it, and he drew her into the curve of his body. "Well, come on, sweetheart. Let's see how well you do now that I've had some time to get myself together."

"Yes," she said. "Let's."

She laughed up into his face but he could feel a tremor run through her.

Hours later, he could actually see her shaking. He wasn't surprised. He'd played without mercy. The others had long ago folded. They were watching what was happening with the fascination of rabbits watching a weasel in their hutch.

Sean had won or intimidated them all. There were half a million dollars worth of chips piled in the middle of the table. He'd just added the hundred thousand that had brought the chips to that amount.

His cards were good. Savannah's were, too. He could tell by the way she ran her fingers over them.

Now she had two choices. Meet his bet and call, or fold.

He knew, with every instinct he possessed, she couldn't afford to fold. He also knew she didn't have any more money.

She had something else, though. And he was going to force her to risk it.

"Well?" He smiled at her. "What's it going to be, sugar?"

She looked at the chips, then at him. They'd gathered a crowd by now. Even high-stakes players had never seen a game quite like this.

"I don't—" She cleared her throat. "I don't have..." She looked around her, as if money might drop from the sky. "I'll give the casino a chit."

Sean's teeth showed in a hungry smile. "No chits here. Check, if you like, but those are the house rules."

"Then—then surely you'll take my personal note, Mr. O'Connell."

"My, oh my, just listen to that. We're back to the 'Mr. O'Connell' thing again." Sean leaned forward. "Sorry, Just-Savannah. I don't take personal notes."

"I told you, I don't have—"

"But you do," he said softly.

"I do?" Her gaze flickered to her wrist and the diamond watch linked around it. "My watch," she said breathlessly. "It's worth—"

"It's worth zero. What would I do with that watch?" Sean let his eyes slip over her, doing it slowly, from her face to her breasts and then back. She was pale and for one second, he felt sorry for her.

Then he remembered why she was here and who had sent her, who owned her, and his heart turned to ice.

"Make it something worth my while."

"I told you, I don't have—"

"Yeah," he said, and he could hear the anger, the hunger, damn it, in his voice. "One night."

"What?"

"I said, if you can't come up with the money, I'll take a night with you in its place."

The crowd stirred, a whisper of shock and delight rushing through it like the wind through a stand of trees.

"You mean—you mean—"

"I mean," Sean said coldly, "you win, the money's yours." He paused, drawing it out for all it was worth, trying not to listen to the blood thundering in his ears. "You lose, you come with me." She didn't answer. Anger and his hot, unwanted desire for her drove him on. "You sleep with me, babe. You got that, or you want me to be more direct?"

He could tell that she was holding her breath. Hell, the whole world was holding its breath.

He didn't know what he'd expected from her in response. Fury? Disbelief? She didn't show either. Nothing changed in her expression and when she spoke, it was slowly, with dignity.

"I understand."

It was Sean's turn to hold his breath. "And?"

"And," she said, "I'll see your cards."

She fanned her cards out. Some of the pink had come back to her face; when he didn't say anything, she even smiled. She had reason to smile. She'd been holding a straight flush. The three, four, five, six and seven of hearts were spots of bright color against the green baize.

"Your turn, Mr. O'Connell."

Sean pursed his lips. "You've got one fine hand there, sugar. An excellent hand. No wonder you were willing to make that bet."

The crowd sighed. So did Savannah. Her smile became real as she leaned across the table and began reaching for the chips.

Sean put his hand over hers. "Not so fast," he said softly.

Her eyes met his. Smiling, never looking away from her, he turned over his cards.

The crowd gasped. So did Savannah. Not Sean. He'd known how this would end. He had the ace, king, queen, jack and ten of spades. A royal flush.

Emotion flashed through him, so swift and fierce he knew he'd never felt anything even remotely like it before. He kicked back his chair, ignored the stack of chips and the crowd. He went around the table to Savannah and held out his hand.

An eternity passed. Then she stood up, ignored his outstretched hand and began walking. He moved alongside her, wrapped his arm tightly around her waist and led her into the night.

CHAPTER FIVE

SAVANNAH WANTED TO DIE.

People were staring, whispering behind their hands. Every eye was on her as Sean laced a hard, proprietorial arm around her waist and led her through the casino. The whispers that had started back at the poker table must have spread like wildfire.

Even in this place, where money and excess were as common as grains of sand on the beach, winning a woman on the turn of a card was big news.

She couldn't blame anyone but herself. What a fool she'd been! Sean had toyed with her, letting her win hand after hand. Had she ever been in control of the game, or had he only let her think she was?

She'd gambled for the highest stakes and lost. Lost her sister's future, her future...

Lost to a man in whose bed she would spend the night.

The realization sent a ribbon of terror whipping through her blood. Savannah stumbled and would have fallen if Sean hadn't had his arm around her. His grasp tightened, his hand spread even more possessively over her hip.

"What's the matter, sugar? You having trouble keeping up with me?"

His words were soft; he dipped his head toward hers and she knew those watching would think he was whispering something low and sexy into her ear. But she heard the hard edge in his voice and when she tilted her face up, she saw his eyes glittering like sea-ice.

"No," he said, his smile slow and cruel, "we both know that's not the problem. You can more than keep up. Fact is, you've been ahead of me from the start."

He'd gone from lust to rage in a heartbeat. Why? Did he know something? He couldn't. Alain had planned things so carefully.

Alain.

Her throat constricted as she imagined his reaction when he heard what had happened. Losing to Sean O'Connell hadn't been an option. Alain had made that clear. Right before the tender took her to shore, he'd cupped her chin and lifted her face until their eyes met. He'd smiled, almost the way he used to when he'd first taken her from New Orleans. For the first time in months, the light kiss he dropped on her mouth had not made her shudder.

"A kiss for good luck, *chérie*."

"I'll do my best, Alain."

"*Oui*. I am certain you will." Another smile, but this one so cold it chilled her to the bone. "And if you need more than a good-luck kiss for a talisman, think of your dear sister as you play. That should cheer you on."

The warning had not been subtle. Remembering it, knowing how she'd failed, Savannah stumbled again.

Sean hauled her against his side. "You want me to pick you up and carry you out of here?"

He'd do it, too. It would add to her humiliation and he'd like that, though she didn't know why. And wasn't that funny? It was supposed to have gone the other way around. *She* was to have humiliated *him*.

Savannah reached deep inside herself and summoned up what remained of her pride. She'd be damned if she'd let him know the true depth of her despair.

"Don't push your luck, O'Connell," she snapped. "You won the bet. You didn't win the right to parade me around like a trophy."

"But that's what you are, sugar." A tight smile flashed across his face. "It's what you were meant to be. A prize I'd want so badly I'd think with my hormones instead of my head."

A cold hand seemed to close around her heart. Was that the explanation for his change in attitude? Was what she'd done so obvious?

"Surprised I figured it out?"

"I don't know what you're talking about."

"No. Of course you don't. You need an explanation, I'll give it to you when we get to my hotel room. For now, just keep moving."

That was all right with her. The sooner they left this place, the better. Anything to get away from the stares and smirks, the soft trills of laughter. The tragic part was that there was nothing funny in what was happening.

Alain's plan had failed. O'Connell hadn't been fooled by her brazen display of sexuality. It hadn't been her fault but Alain wouldn't see it that way. He'd lay the blame on her.

Yes, she'd changed things by telling Sean she wanted to play against him, but she hadn't had much choice. It hadn't bothered him. If anything, he'd seemed amused by her admission.

It had all gone so smoothly at first. She'd played as well as she ever had, better, really, because she knew how high the stakes were. And Alain's predictions had been correct. O'Connell was too busy watching her to pay attention to the game. She'd won and won and won—well, except for that time his interest seemed to be waning. She'd folded early and let him win.

Things had been going just fine... Until that break.

All the others at the table had wanted to take a breather. She had to give in. What else could she have done? The last thing she'd wanted was to call attention to herself.

But she hadn't wanted to give O'Connell time to think, either. She'd thought of an easy solution. All she had to do was ask him to go with her. Step out on the terrace for some air. There, in the warm, sea-scented darkness, she could have smiled up at him from under her lashes. Tossed back her head when she laughed. Men liked looking at her when she did that. She won because of her skill at poker when she played for Alain, but that didn't mean she'd never noticed the hot male eyes that took in her every motion.

And yet, she hadn't done it. Something about the idea of being alone in the night with him again had made her feel... What? Uncomfortable? Uneasy? Maybe it was because she didn't like knowing she was cheating him, even though he deserved it. Maybe it was because she wanted to win as much on ability as she could.

Maybe it was because the thought of being alone in the dark with Sean made her pulse quicken. Things could happen between a man and a woman on a warm tropical night. He might reach for her. Draw her into his arms. Take her mouth in a slow, drugging kiss.

It was hard enough, playing at seduction, promising something she had no intention of delivering. She'd fled to the ladies' lounge, let cold water run over her wrists, then called Alain on her cell phone to tell him how well things were going.

And jinxed herself.

She'd sensed a change in Sean as soon as he led her back to the table. The Texan had started to say something but Sean's sharp voice silenced him.

"Let's not waste time," he'd said. "Just play the game."

A couple of minutes later, she'd known it was all over.

Her adversary was playing with a single-minded intensity that was frightening, and exhibiting a level of skill and daring that made it clear he was out for blood.

He showed no mercy. A desire for something more than winning was fueling him.

Each time he looked at her, she saw rage in his eyes.

Smart players knew when to call it quits. Under normal circumstances she'd have bowed out but nothing about this night was normal. She *had* to win. So she'd kept playing. She won a couple of small pots, but she lost big each time it came down to only O'Connell and her until the others were simply spectators at what had become a blood sport.

Eventually, she'd stared disaster in the face. She was out of money. Every dollar Alain had given her was gone. No options left except going back to Alain and admitting failure. Then that terrible moment, Sean looking at her and in an impassive voice offering her a final, desperate chance...

"Get in the car."

Savannah looked up, startled. Somehow, they were out of the casino. A low-slung black sports car stood purring at the curb. A valet held the passenger door open.

The full reality of what awaited her was a dagger of ice straight to the heart. She was going to bed with a stranger. With a man who'd taken to looking at her as if she were something that had crawled out of a sewer.

Her steps faltered. "Wait a minute."

"Are you going to welsh on the bet, McRae?"

He'd called her by her name, but she'd never given it to him. *God, oh God, oh God!*

"Get in the car. If you walk away, I'll make sure there's not a casino in the world that will let you in the door."

She stared at him. His face was a mask of contained rage. Why? What did he know? Better still, what choice did she have? She could go with him or go to Alain.

Either way, she was lost.

Numb, Savannah did as he'd commanded. The valet shut the door. Sean got behind the wheel. "Fasten your seat belt."

She almost laughed. Who gave a damn what happened to her now? If the car went off a cliff and into the sea, what would it matter?

He muttered something, leaned over and reached for the ends of the belt. His hand brushed across her breasts. To her horror, she felt them lift, felt her nipples harden. He knew it, too. He stopped what he was doing and looked into her eyes and then, with slow insolence, at her breasts. He smiled when their eyes met again but this time, the smile didn't chill her to the bone.

It made her think.

Whatever O'Connell knew or thought he knew, he had no right to sit in judgment on her. He was a cheat and a thief. She wasn't either one.

As for losing… Yes. She had. But Alain wasn't an animal. She'd explain things to him. He wouldn't make good on his threats about Missy. No. He wouldn't do that to her. They'd sit down together, come up with a better plan to defeat Sean O'Connell.

In the meantime, she wouldn't let O'Connell see her fear. She'd do what she had to do, the way she used to on the New Orleans streets long ago.

She'd learned to block out the real world with a better world inside her head. Think of a million other things so she didn't have to think about her empty belly or her sister's soft weeping or the brush of a rat's tail as it ran across her legs while she and Missy slept huddled together in a doorway.

All those hard-earned skills would save her tonight. Sean O'Connell would claim his prize. He'd do what men did to women in bed. And she—she wouldn't be there. Not really. She'd be inside her own thoughts where there was no fear, no panic, no pain.

He'd won her body, but she'd never let him take her soul.

SEAN'S HOTEL was on the southern coast of Emeraude, far from the casinos and the glitter that drew the rich and famous of the world.

The hotel was a former plantation house restored to glory by the whim and wealth of a deposed European prince. One look at the elegant suites, the quiet beaches and coves, and Sean had known he'd never stay anywhere else when he was on this island. The place was a half-hour drive from the busy casinos and that had always seemed a fine thing. It gave him time to unwind as he headed home.

Tonight, he was sorry for the delay.

Damn it, he was angry. Angry? He choked back a laugh as he took his Porsche through the hairpin curves that wound along the coast. Hell, no. He wasn't angry. He was enraged. It had been all he could do to play out the game. To keep from reaching across the table, dragging Savannah from her chair, shaking her until her teeth rattled...

Kissing her until she begged him to stop.

He wouldn't have stopped. No way. She'd been set out as bait, and bait was expendable.

What kind of woman would use herself to break a man's bank account? What kind of woman would be Alain Beaumont's mistress? Sleep in his bed, turn her naked body into his arms, let him run his slimy hands over her soft flesh?

Sean gritted his teeth.

A woman who'd bet one night with a stranger against the stakes in a card game.

Headlights appeared in the darkness. The road was narrow, narrower still along this last stretch that led to his hotel.

Normally, he'd slow his speed, pull the car over toward the scrub palmetto and wild beach grasses that lined the verge. Not tonight. Instead, he stepped down harder on the gas. The horn of the oncoming vehicle blasted as Sean roared by. He mouthed an oath and drove faster.

Who gave a damn about safety tonight?

Not him. Jesus, not him! He'd been taken in by a woman with hair of gold and eyes of jade, a woman whose soft, pink mouth he'd imagined savoring the minute he'd first seen her. Her kiss had shaken him as no other woman's ever had.

And she was a pawn owned by a piece of scum like Beaumont.

But he'd come out the winner. He'd taken Beaumont's money once again. Now he'd take his woman as well. He'd use her every way a man could, until those big eyes glittered with tears of shame, until that sweet-looking mouth was swollen and her thighs trembled because he'd spread them so many times.

No way she'd be thinking about her pig of a lover by then.

The tires clawed for control as he made a sharp turn into the hotel's circular drive. The parking valet trotted up and opened Sean's door as he shut off the engine. The boy smiled and greeted him but Sean wasn't in the mood for pleasantries. He brushed by the kid and flung open Savannah's door before the doorman could get there.

"Get out."

The soft glow of the interior lights illuminated her face. She was as pale as death except for two red streaks along her cheeks. The valet threw him a surprised look. Sean didn't give a damn. All that mattered was getting his pound of flesh.

"Out," he said again, and bent toward her. She pulled

back, her face becoming even whiter as he reached toward her seat belt. She wasn't stupid, he thought grimly. She'd learned the limits of his patience and she didn't want him to touch her again.

Had the instant of awareness when he'd brushed his hand over her breast been part of the game, or had she actually responded to his touch? Sean narrowed his eyes. It had been an act, the same as everything else. Savannah McRae was Alain Beaumont's toy.

Tonight, she would be his.

He tossed the valet a bill, clasped Savannah's arm and hurried her up the wide marble steps to the lobby. Only one clerk was at the reception desk at this time of night. He smiled politely when he saw Sean but his eyebrows rose at the sight of Savannah. Women in too-short red dresses, wearing heels that made the most of their up-to-their-ears legs, weren't the standard here.

"Mr. O'Connell," the clerk said politely, his composure regained. "Good evening, sir."

"Edward." Sean looked at the man. "I'd ask you to have room service send up some champagne, but we won't need it. Will we, sugar?" He shot Savannah a smile he knew was all teeth. "Why waste a bottle of good wine when it's not necessary?"

Savannah paled. The clerk turned crimson. Good, Sean thought savagely. Two birds with one stone.

He tugged her toward the elevator. Once inside, he put his key in the lock that would take them up to the penthouse. She tried to pull away but he had a grip of steel.

"What's the matter, sugar? Not in the mood? I can't believe that. Not after the big come-on earlier."

She didn't answer. Damn it, why not? He wanted her to say something. To plead with him to forget their bet, or at least to ask him to treat her with courtesy.

The elevator doors opened; he hurried her straight through the sitting room and into a bedroom overlooking the sea.

Sean kicked the door closed and turned the lock. And that—the sound of the bolt clicking home—finally changed the expression on Savannah's beautiful face.

What he saw there was fear.

For a heartbeat, the fury inside him subsided. He wanted to go to her, take her in his arms, tell her he wouldn't hurt her, that he'd be gentle, make slow love to her until she was sobbing with pleasure...

"Unlock the door."

The words, almost whispered, brought him back to sanity. He'd almost forgotten how good she was at acting.

"Relax, sugar. I'm just seeing to it we aren't disturbed."

"We made a bet. I'm prepared to go through with it but—"

"But?" he said, cocking his head as if he really gave a damn what she said next.

"But..." She swallowed, caught her lip between her teeth. "But I won't—I won't do anything—anything—"

"Kinky?" He grinned, shrugged off his jacket and tossed it aside. "Oh, I think you will, Just-Savannah. In fact, I'm willing to bet on it."

He watched her breasts rise and fall as she took a deep breath, then exhaled. Color was returning to her face. If he hadn't known better, he'd have sworn she was willing herself to be strong, but that was crazy.

A woman who slept with Alain Beaumont would sleep with anybody, even a man who won her at a poker table.

"You'd lose that bet, O'Connell."

Sean shrugged his shoulders. "No problem, babe. You give me whatever you give your lover and we'll call it even."

"My lover?"

Oh, she was good! That look, the total innocence in her eyes, even the surprise in her voice... She was better than good. She was great.

Would she be that great in bed? Yes. Oh, yes, she would be. Sean could almost taste her mouth. Her nipples would be honey on his tongue, her belly would have the scent of vanilla when he kissed it. Her golden thighs would carry the clean, erotic scent of a woman aroused as he parted them to reveal the hidden essence of her.

God, he was hard as stone.

"Yeah," he said gruffly as he started toward her. "Your lover. Beaumont. Remember him?"

"I didn't—he isn't—"

Sean reached her. He looped one hand around her throat. She flinched but stood her ground. He could feel the hammer of her pulse beneath his fingers. Slowly, he ran his hand over her, lightly cupping her breast, then curving it over her hip.

"Stop lying. You didn't learn to play cards on a riverboat. Alain Beaumont taught you."

"I don't know what you're talking ab—"

She gasped as he put both arms around her and drew her up against him. He knew she could feel his erection. Hell, he'd never been this hard in his life.

"What else did Beaumont teach you, sugar?"

The idea of lying flashed through her mind. Sean could almost see her thought process.

"Come on," he growled. "Be honest just once tonight. Admit he's your lover, that he put you up to this, that you were supposed to take me down and walk away laughing."

She didn't answer. Sean cursed, pulled her to her toes and crushed her mouth beneath his. She gave a sob that pierced his heart before he remembered this was all a game. She was playing a part. Nothing more, nothing less.

"Admit it," he said roughly. "Beaumont put you on to me."

Tears glittered in her eyes. "You stole from him."

"I what?"

"Stole. Cheated him out of a million dollars. In a card game on his yacht."

"That's one terrific story, sugar."

"It's the truth!"

"Let me get this straight. I stole a million bucks from your lover and you decided to steal it back to get even?"

"I wasn't trying to steal your money. I was winning it in a poker game."

"You were winning only because you kept me so busy looking at you that I couldn't think straight."

"That's not true! I'm a good poker player."

"Right. You're so good that you lost your lover's stake and ended with nothing to put on the table but yourself." Sean took a step back. "And now it's time to deliver."

"Sean. Mr. O'Connell…" Savannah heard the sudden desperation in her voice. No. She'd promised she wouldn't let him see her fear or hear her beg… but Lord, how could she do this? Give herself to a man who despised her? Let him touch her, explore her, take the last of her innocence, the only innocence she'd been able to hang on to in her life?

He was leaning against the dresser, arms folded over his chest, feet crossed at the ankles, watching her with no expression at all on his face. He was a thief, yes, but he wasn't unkind. Another man might have laughed and dismissed her when she'd told him that lie about why she wanted to play against him.

He hadn't. He'd listened.

Maybe he'd listen now.

"Mr. O'Connell." Savannah moistened her lips. "There's—there's been a misunderstanding. I—I wasn't thinking straight when I agreed to—"

"Strip."

She blanched. "Please. If you'd just hear me out—"

"Are you going to pay me the money that you lost to me tonight?"

"I can't. But—but—"

But what? She owed him a small fortune. She didn't have the money to pay it. She never would. And Alain would never give it to her, either. It was bad enough she'd return to him in defeat. She couldn't return and ask him for money, too.

"Either pay me the money or start getting undressed. Take your time about it. I want to enjoy the show."

Sean waited, hardly breathing. What would she do next? Run for her life, probably. Make a dash for the door, fumble with the lock and, damn it, he'd let her get away. He wanted her, yes. Why lie to himself? He wanted her badly, but not this way.

He couldn't go through with this. Even if she was willing, he'd—he'd—

The slow movement of her arms as she reached behind her stopped his thinking. His heart hammered as she slid down the zipper of the sexy red dress. One strap drooped against her shoulder, then the other. Her head was down but she must have felt his eyes on her because she lifted her chin and looked at him.

What he saw on her face almost killed him.

Here I am, she was saying. *Do what you will. Take what you want. It doesn't matter. I won't feel anything you do to me.*

But she would. He'd make her feel. He'd make her know

it was his hands on her, not Beaumont, that she was in his bed, not anyone else's.

Eyes still on his, she began to ease off one of those incredible shoes. Sean cleared his throat.

"Leave them on," he said hoarsely. "Take off the dress and leave the rest."

She took a deep breath and the red silk slithered to the carpet. She was wearing a black lace bra that cupped her breasts as lovingly as a man's hands, a black lace thong that covered that part of her that was all female, thigh-high, sheer-as-a-whisper black stockings and those shoes.

She was the most beautiful woman he'd ever seen and, for tonight, she belonged to him. He'd make her forget everything else.

He walked toward her slowly. The tears trembling on her lashes might have gotten to him if he hadn't reminded himself that they were about as real as the rest of her act.

"Beaumont is a lucky man," he said. She didn't answer. Sean trailed a finger down her throat, skimmed the curve of her breasts. "You're a feast for the eyes, Savannah. Do you taste as good as you look?"

She was shaking. Hell, he thought coldly, she was incredibly good at this. He clasped her face, lifted it to him, intending to brand her with his kiss. Instead, he found himself brushing his lips over hers, gently, softly, groaning at the sweetness of her mouth.

Everything he'd been thinking fled his mind. He drew her close and kissed her, again and again, until she made a sound deep in her throat. Her hands came up, touched his chest, slid up to his shoulders. She was weeping silently now, her tears leaving glittering streaks down her silken cheeks.

It was the tears that did it.

The ice around Sean's heart melted. Savannah was afraid

of him. How could this be an act? She was terrified, but she didn't have anything to fear. He wouldn't hurt her. He'd be gentle, stroke her with slow hands, kiss her until she clung to him with desire.

"Savannah," he whispered. "Don't cry. I won't hurt you. Let me show you. Let me."

He kissed her again, still with tenderness even though he wanted more, wanted her with a ferocity that shocked him. He held back with a strength he'd never known he possessed. When her mouth began to soften and cling to his, he nipped lightly at her bottom lip until she sighed. Then, slowly, he eased the tip of his tongue into her mouth. She made that little sound, the one she'd made before, and tried to twist her face away but he wouldn't let her. He held her, kissed her, whispered to her until she began to melt in his arms.

She wanted him.

The knowledge hit him like a thunderbolt. She wanted him.

Sean murmured her name and bent her back over his arm. He buried his lips in the sweet softness of her throat, cupped the high curve of her breast and caught her lace-covered nipple between his teeth.

Savannah moaned his name.

And then sanity returned.

What in hell was he doing? Of course this was an act. The woman in his arms was giving an Oscar-winning performance and he was letting himself get sucker-punched all over again.

He let go of her, shoved her away. She stumbled; her eyes flew open, and for one impossible second he let himself believe that what he saw in their depths was confusion. But she could make him see whatever she wanted. She had, from the minute he'd laid eyes on her.

Sean snarled an oath as he snatched up her dress and flung it at her. She caught it and clutched it to her breasts.

"Get out!"

"But—but I thought—"

"Yeah. I know what you thought." His mouth twisted. "You thought wrong, sugar. I don't take another man's leavings." He took a step toward her, dug a handful of bills from his pocket and flung them at her feet. "Here's cab fare. Go back to Beaumont and tell him you still owe me. Tell him I'll come around one of these days to teach him a lesson he should have learned the last time we met."

He strode into the bathroom and slammed the door. When he opened it again, the bills still lay scattered on the carpet.

Savannah was gone.

CHAPTER SIX

WHAT DID A MAN DO to work off his anger when he couldn't get the woman who was the cause of it out of his head?

Sean paced like a caged lion. He took a shower so long and cold he risked frostbite. He grabbed the prior day's newspaper and flipped the pages without reading a word.

And yet, all he could do was think about Savannah and how she'd scammed him. He was a gambler, for God's sake. He'd seen people pull a thousand cons. Making it seem you were doing one thing while you were really planning another was at the heart of the game he played best.

But he'd never come up against a woman like this before.

What an ass he'd been. He'd known a lot of beautiful women in his life—too many, probably. He'd always been able to see past the lovely faces, the toned bodies, and figure out what they really wanted.

Not tonight. Savannah had pushed his buttons and gotten what she wanted.

And what had he been thinking, that he hadn't collected on their wager? Forget her tears. They'd been as phony as everything else about her. A bet was a bet. If he'd taken her to bed, he wouldn't be so damned angry now. The whole nasty episode would be behind him. He'd be done with that soft mouth. The silken skin. Those rounded breasts and endless legs. Done with her.

He flung the newspaper aside.

The hell he would.

If he'd had her once, he'd have wanted her again. All through the night, through the first flush of dawn. Once wouldn't have been enough, not for him, not for her.

Yes, the weeping, the trembling, had been part of the act. But maybe that little sob of passion, the way she'd melted against him, had been real. Maybe she'd really felt something when he touched her. Maybe…

Sean cursed in disgust. What pure, unadulterated bull. The lady hadn't felt a thing, except when she was winning. When he was *letting* her win. That was another reason he was so furious, not just at her but at himself. She'd played him for the worst kind of jerk, he'd let it happen, and she'd done it for Beaumont, the lying, cheating son of a bitch!

Okay. It was too late to change what had happened, but not too late to get even. Alain Beaumont would pay. So would Savannah. What was that old saying about revenge being a dish best served cold? Sean smiled with grim amusement. The time would come. He'd find a way. Until then, all he had to do was be patient.

Too bad patience wasn't in his nature.

He pulled on a pair of trunks, went down to the dark beach and plunged into the surf. He swam out beyond the breakers, swam out farther than any intelligent man would, but then he had no claim on intelligence, not after tonight. Under the cool gaze of the setting moon, he floated on his back in the warm sea until, finally, he felt the tension drain away.

When he returned to his suite, he fell into a deep, exhausted sleep.

THE RING OF HIS CELL PHONE jolted him awake.

Sean sat up and peered at his watch. It was four-fifteen. Nobody phoned with good news at this hour. Dozens of possibilities ran through his mind but when he heard his older brother say, "Kid, it's me," he knew that the news was the worst it could be.

"Is it Ma?" he asked hoarsely. "Another heart attack?"

"No," Keir said, but Sean's relief was short-lived. "A stroke."

The bed seemed to tilt. Sean swung his feet to the floor. "Is she—is she—"

"She's still with us, but I won't mince words. The doctors don't know how things are going to go."

The heart attack had almost killed their mother. If Keir was saying this was worse...

No. Sean wasn't going there. If Mary Elizabeth was alive, there was still hope.

"Where is she? Vegas? Same place as last time?"

"She's in New York. Mount Sinai Hospital, cardiac care ICU. She and Dan were on vacation when it happened."

"I'm on my way. I'll see you in..." Sean checked the time again and did some quick calculations. "Four hours."

"Right. Cull's here, and the girls, and—"

"Keir?"

"Yeah, kid?"

"Tell her I'm coming, okay? And that I love her."

"She doesn't..." Keir cleared his throat. "Sure. Sure, I'll tell her."

"Will she—do the doctors think—" Sean's voice broke.

"Just hurry," Keir said, and hung up the phone.

Sean sat still for a long moment. Then he punched in the number of a company that leased private jets. Forty minutes later, he was on his way to the States.

HOSPITALS ALL SMELLED the same. Not that Sean had been in many, but you remembered from one time to the next. Antiseptic. Disinfectant. Lots of both, as if they could cover up the stench of pain, despair and death.

Mary Elizabeth O'Connell-Coyle lay motionless on a bed in the cardiac care ICU. Sean's heart lurched when he saw her. His mother was a beautiful woman. Not now. Her normally ruddy face was white, her eyes were shut and her once-firm mouth was slack. Tubes ran from under the white cotton blanket that covered her to a stand holding bottles that dripped fluids into them. A tangle of thin wires led to a panel of blinking lights on a monitor.

He couldn't stop watching those lights. They marked his mother's continuing struggle to hang on to life.

He sat beside her, clutching her hand, talking to her in a soft voice, telling her how much he loved her, how he needed her, how they all needed her. Then he waited, hoped, prayed for a response. Anything. It didn't have to be much. A squeeze of her fingers. A flicker of the eyelid. He'd have settled for that.

The only things that changed were the nurses who came and went. They checked the tubes, straightened the linen, did things that didn't really mean a damn when what he wanted was someone to come in and announce they'd found a cure for her ailing heart, a magic potion that would make her young and whole again.

"Sean?"

He blinked back his tears and looked up at his brother, Cullen, who put a comforting hand on his shoulder.

"I know you just got here," Cull said, "but—"

"But everyone else wants to be with her, too." Sean nodded and got to his feet. "Sure. I understand."

Of course he understood. They were allowed into the cubicle for fifteen minutes each. Multiply those scant quarter hours by a husband and six children. Add two sons-in-law and the same number of daughters-in-law, and you could see that there just wasn't enough time.

There'd never be enough time.

His throat constricted as he leaned down and kissed his mother's pallid cheek. He and Cullen exchanged quick embraces. Then he went into the ICU waiting room and hugged the rest of the O'Connell clan before settling into an imitation leather armchair that looked as worn and weary as the room's occupants.

All they could do now was wait.

IN LATE AFTERNOON, his sisters went to the cafeteria and brought back sandwiches that might or might not have been edible. Nobody knew because nobody could manage more than a bite. Keir bought out all the candy bars in the vending machine; Cullen fed dollar bills into the maw of a contraption that promised coffee but oozed sludge. They all gulped it down, mostly because it gave them something to do. Nobody needed the caffeine. Though they hovered on the brink of exhaustion, sleep remained as elusive as good news.

Their stepfather told them he'd rented a large suite in a nearby hotel. "Get some rest," Dan urged. "What good will any of us be to Mary if we're out on our feet when she awakens?"

When, not if. They clung to the subtle message, nodded in agreement, but nobody left. After a while, Dan went back into the ICU to be with his wife. Sean watched his sisters, Megan and Fallon, lean against their husbands. He saw Keir put his arm around his wife and smile wearily when she laid her hand against his cheek, saw Cullen press a kiss to his wife's forehead as she whispered to him.

Only Sean and his kid sister, Briana, were alone.

Bree must have read his thoughts. She rose from her chair, crossed the room and sat next to him.

"Only you and me left," she said, with a little smile. "Everyone else got hitched."

Sean managed a smile in return. "Who'd a thunk it?"

Bree gave a deep sigh. "Guess it must be nice to have somebody at a time like this, though, don't you think?"

A face flashed through Sean's mind. A woman with cascading hair the colors of gold and caramel, and eyes as green as the sea. The image shook him and he pushed it away.

"We do have somebody," he said gruffly. "We have each other."

His sister took his hand and squeezed it. "Sean? You think Ma will be all right?"

"She'll be fine," he said with more conviction than he felt, and he put his arm around Briana and hugged her tight.

HOURS PASSED. Daylight faded and it was night again.

The men gathered in the hall for a whispered consultation. When they stepped into the waiting room, they all had the same determined look.

Sean nodded toward his two brothers-in-law. "Stefano and Qasim are going to the hotel," he told his sisters. "They're taking you ladies with them."

There was a blur of protest. The men held fast.

"No arguments," Cullen said firmly.

The women rose reluctantly. Sean turned to Dan.

"Come on," he said to his stepfather, and used Dan's own earlier words. "Ma's going to need you when she regains consciousness. You'll have to be here, one hundred percent."

Again, it was when, not if. They were all taking strength from that. Dan gave a reluctant nod. "I'll do it, but only so I can give your mother my opinion of the hotel. She always likes to know what the competition's doing."

It was a forlorn attempt at humor but they grabbed it like a lifeline, especially since it was a reminder of Mary Elizabeth's vitality as head of the Desert Song Hotel in Las Vegas. Keir, Cullen and Sean promised to phone if there was the slightest change and yes, of course, they'd take a breather themselves in a few hours.

When the others had gone, the brothers sat in silence for a while. Then Sean cleared his throat.

"How did it happen?"

Cullen and Keir shook their heads. "It just did," Cull said. "Dan and Ma were in Central Park. He says they were walking along, talking…"

"About what? Was she upset over something?"

"No, she wasn't upset. She was talking about you and Bree."

"About Briana and me?"

"Yeah. The usual thing. You know, how she'd be happy if Bree would find a guy to love, and if you'd get married and settle down."

"What do you mean, 'the usual thing'?" Sean frowned. "Ma never said—"

"Well," Cullen said uncomfortably, "she wouldn't. Not to you, but to us, you know, she says she worries about you guys, that you're alone."

"No," Sean said tightly. "I don't know. And if you're trying to tell me that's why she had—that I'm the reason for—"

"Settle down, little brother," Keir said quickly. "Nobody's even suggesting that. You asked what she was talking about. We're telling you."

Sean glared at his brothers. Then his face crumpled. "Right. I know that's not why this happened. It's only that—that it's hard to—to—"

"Yeah," Cullen said, "it is."

"What about the doctors?"

"They're doing everything they can."

"Did you call in a consultant? I know this guy's supposed to be top-notch, but—"

"He *is* top-notch," Cullen said quietly.

"We flew in Ma's own doctor," Keir added. "He agreed on her treatment."

Sean sprang to his feet. "Treatment? What treatment? She's lying in that bed. I don't call that treatment, I call that—"

"They gave her a drug. It's supposed to dissolve the clot that's causing the problem."

Problem? Sean almost laughed. That was a hell of a way to describe something that might kill their mother.

"Sean." Keir stood up and put an arm around his younger brother. "We're all going nuts here, but we have to wait. It's all we can do."

Sean's shoulders sagged. "You're right. It's just—"

He sat down. So did Keir. The three O'Connells were silent for a long time. Then Cullen mouthed an oath.

"I hate this place," he growled.

"Take a walk," Keir told him. "Get some air. Go around the block."

"No. No, I want to be here if—when…" Cullen fell silent, struggling for self-control. "Hey," he said, his tone as artificial as the flowers on a corner table, "did I tell you guys that Marissa and I drove down from Boston and took Ma and Dan to dinner the other night?"

He was, Sean knew, trying to change the subject, which was probably a damned fine idea. Okay. He'd do his part.

"Smart woman, our mother," he said briskly. "Won't catch her risking ptomaine by having a meal at Big Brother's la-ti-da restaurant in Connecticut."

Keir forced out a laugh. "Hey, kid. Just because you wouldn't know haute cuisine from hamburger doesn't mean the rest of the family has no taste. Ma and Dan came up for supper with us and stayed the night as soon as they hit the city.''

"Only because Marissa and I didn't get into town until the next day," Cullen said.

"Yeah," Sean added, "and what's with that crack about my taste buds?"

"It wasn't a crack," Keir said. "It was the truth. There we were, growing up with room service ready to provide anything from beef Wellington to lobster thermidor, and what did you ask for, night after night? A cheeseburger and fries."

"Oh, not *every* night," Cullen said. "Our little brother used to cleanse his palate with an occasional hot dog."

"They were chili dogs," Sean said, "and did you really just say 'cleanse his palate'?"

"What can I tell you? I've got a wife who decided she loves to cook. She gets these magazines, you know? And sometimes I leaf through them."

Sean looked at Keir. "Cullen's learned to read," he said solemnly.

"Miracles happen," Keir replied.

Miracles. Would one happen in this hospital tonight? The same thought hit them all and ended their forced attempt at levity. Sean tried to think of something to talk about but came up empty. Keir was the one who made the next try at conversation.

"So," he said, "where were you when I phoned?"

Sean looked up. "Emeraude Island. In the Bahamas."

"Nice?"

"Yeah."

More silence. Cullen cleared his throat. "Marissa and I've been thinking of getting away for a long weekend. What's Emeraude like?"

"You know. Pink sand beaches. Blue water. Lush mountains."

"And casinos."

"A couple."

"How'd you do?"

Sean stretched out his legs and crossed them at the ankles. "Okay."

"Okay, he says." Cullen raised his eyebrows. "What'd you win this time? A trillion bucks?"

"No."

"My God," Keir said, "don't tell me. You lost!"

"I didn't say that."

"Well, that's how you made it sound." He smiled. "How much did you win, then?"

Sean gave a shrug. "A few hundred thousand."

"And that wasn't enough to make you happy?"

No, Sean thought in mild surprise, it wasn't.

"Kid? What's the matter?"

A muscle knotted in Sean's jaw. "I won something else."

"Ah. No, don't tell us. Let me guess. A car? A yacht?" Keir grinned at Cullen. "A French chateau?"

"A woman," Sean said flatly.

His brothers' jaws dropped. "A what?"

"You heard me. I won a—"

"Mr. O'Connell?"

The O'Connells sprang to their feet. Sean could feel his heart trying to pound its way out of his chest until he saw the smile on the face of the nurse who'd come into the room. They all let out a breath in one big whoosh.

"Your mother's regained consciousness, gentlemen." Her smile broadened. "And because she won't have it any other way, the doctor's agreed to let her visit with all of you at once."

MARY ELIZABETH WAS BACK.

Maybe not completely. After a week, she was still paler than anyone liked, still looking fragile. Her speech was a little slurred and there were times she had to search for words.

But her smile was the same as it had always been. Her sense of humor was intact. So was her determination to take charge, even from a hospital bed.

She insisted Dan had to fly home and oversee things at the Desert Song. She told Cullen and Marissa it was more important they be at home with their baby than here with her, and tried to shoo Keir and Cassie away with the same message. She gave marching orders to Fallon and Stefano, then to Megan and Qasim.

Yes, they all said, yes, of course, absolutely, they'd leave.

Nobody did.

In the end, the only people she didn't try to boss around were Briana and Sean. It was, she said, lovely having her youngest daughter nearby. And when she and Sean were alone, she told him it was better to know he was here than to imagine him wasting his time at a card table.

Sean knew his mother had never really approved of the way he lived but she'd never come out and said so before. He was surprised by her candor and she knew it.

"It's what a little glimpse of your own mortality does to you," she told him as he sat with her in the hospital's roof-top conservatory one afternoon. "A mother should speak bluntly to her favorite son."

Sean smiled. "I'll bet you say the same thing to Keir and Cullen."

"Of course," Mary said, smiling back at him. "You're all my favorites." Her smile dimmed. "But I worry about you the most. After all, you're my baby."

Sean raised his mother's hand to his mouth and kissed her knuckles. "I'm thirty years old," he said gently.

"Exactly."

"I'm almost disgustingly healthy."

"Good."

"And I'm happy."

"That's what you think."

"It's what I know, Ma. Trust me. I'm happy."

Mary shook her head. "You're a gambler."

"I like gambling. I'm not addicted to it," he said, smiling at his mother, "if that's what you mean. I can stop whenever I want."

"But you don't."

"Because I enjoy it. You should understand that. Pa was a gambler."

Mary nodded. "He was, indeed," she said quietly. "It was the one thing about him that broke my heart."

Sean stared at her. "I thought—"

"Oh, I loved your father, Sean. Loved him deeply." She sighed. "But I wish he'd loved me more than the cards."

"Ma, for heaven's sake, he worshiped you!"

"He did, yes, in his own way, but if I'd been enough for him, he'd have settled down. Made a real home for us. You remember how bad it was, the years before we stumbled on to the Desert Song." Mary clasped her youngest son's hand and looked deep into his eyes. "A man should find his happiness in a woman, not in the turn of a card."

"We're not all the same, Ma. What's good for Cull and Keir isn't necessarily right for me."

His mother sighed. After a minute, she squeezed his hand. "My birthday's the week after next."

"Your..."

"My birthday, yes. And don't look at me as if I've slipped 'round the bend, Sean O'Connell. I can change the subject without being daft, though I'm not really changing the subject. I'm just thinking how quickly life slips by."

"Ma—"

"Let me talk, Sean. Why shouldn't we admit the truth? I almost died."

"Yes." A hand seemed to close around his heart. "But you didn't," he said fiercely. "That's what counts."

"Lying in that bed, drifting in that place halfway between this world and the next, I kept thinking, 'It's too soon.'"

"Much too soon," Sean said gruffly.

"I don't want to leave this earth until all my children are happy."

"I *am* happy, Ma. You don't need to worry about it."

"You're alone, Sean."

"Times have changed. A person doesn't need to be married to be happy."

"A person needs to love and be loved. That hasn't changed. You have your father's itchy foot and his gift for the cards, but that can't make up for the love of a good woman."

Unbidden, a face swam into Sean's mind. Green eyes. A mane of golden hair. A soft mouth tasting like berries warmed by the sun. It was the face of a woman a man would burn to possess, but love? Never. Thinking of Savannah McRae and the word "good" at the same time was absurd.

Besides, his mother was wrong. A man didn't need love. He needed freedom. His father had loved his wife and children but Sean suspected he'd have been happier without them. In his heart, he was the same. It was the one bond he and his old man had shared.

"I know you think you're right, Ma," he said gently, "but I like my life as it is." He smiled. "You want to be a matchmaker, why not take on Briana?"

"Bree will find somebody," Mary said with conviction. "She just needs a little more time. But you..."

"I'll give it some serious thought," Sean said, trying to sound sincere even if he was lying through his teeth, but it was a white lie, and white lies didn't count. "Maybe, someday, when I meet the right woman."

Mary sighed. "I just hope I live long enough to see it happen."

"You'll be here for years and years."

"Nobody can see the future," his mother said softly.

What could he say to that? Sean swallowed hard, searched for a change of subject and finally found one.

"That birthday—"

"Ah, yes. Dan and I want to have a big party."

"Not too much, though. You need peace and quiet."

"What I need is to get back into life."

Sean smiled. "You sound as if you're back into it already. And what would you like as a special gift?"

"Just all my children and grandchildren gathered around me."

"Nothing more?" Sean grinned. "Come on, Ma. Tell me your heart's desire and I'll get it for you."

Mary's eyes met his. "You will?"

"Yes. Absolutely. What do you want, hmm? Emeralds from Colombia? Pearls from the South Seas?" He bent forward and kissed her temple. "Name it, Mrs. Coyle, and it'll be yours."

His mother gave him a long look. "Do you mean it?"

"Have I ever made a promise to you and broken it?"

"No. No, you haven't."

"Well, then, tell me what you want for your birthday and you'll have it. Cross my heart and hope to die."

Sean said the words as solemnly as if he were seven years old instead of thirty, and he smiled. But his mother didn't smile. Instead, she looked so deep into his eyes that he felt the hair rise on the nape of his neck.

"I want to see you married, Sean O'Connell," she said. And from the expression on her face, he knew she meant every word.

CHAPTER SEVEN

AMAZING, what a combination of medical science and determination could accomplish. Ten days after Mary O'Connell-Coyle's stroke, her doctors pronounced her well and sent her home.

Keir, Cullen and Sean accompanied Dan and their mother to the airport. They sat with her in the first-class lounge and asked if she wanted anything so many times that Mary finally threw up her hands and said if they didn't stop fussing over her, she was going to go and find a seat in the terminal.

"One seat," she warned, "with no empties nearby." She looked at her husband, who smiled, and smiled back at him. "All right. Two seats, then, but not another within miles."

The brothers looked at each other sheepishly. Then they hugged her and kissed her, waited until the plane that would take her to Vegas had safely lifted off, and headed, by unspoken consent, for a taxi and a quiet, very untrendy bar Keir knew in lower Manhattan.

"My arms hurt," Sean said solemnly. His brothers raised inquisitive eyebrows. "From doing all that lifting to get the plane in the air."

He grinned. His brothers laughed, and Keir raised his glass of ale. "To Ma."

The men touched glasses. They drank, then leaned back in the time-worn leather booth.

"So," Keir said, "I guess we can all head home. Me to

Connecticut, Cull to Boston.'' He looked at Sean. ''You going back to that island?''

Sean felt a muscle knot in his jaw. ''Yes.''

''Can't get enough of the sea and sand?''

''I have unfinished business there.''

''Must be important.''

Getting even was always important, Sean thought coldly. ''Yeah. It is.''

Cullen grinned and nudged Keir with his elbow. ''Something to do with that woman, I bet.''

''What woman?'' Sean said, much too quickly.

''Come on, bro. The babe you won in a game of cards.'' Keir reached for the bowl of peanuts. ''You never did explain that.''

''There's nothing to explain.''

''There's nothing to explain, he says.'' Cullen dug out a handful of nuts, too, and started munching. ''A man wins a night with a hooker, and he says—''

''Did I say she was a hooker?''

Sean's voice was glacial. Cullen and Keir exchanged glances. He could hardly blame them. What was he doing? Defending Savannah's honor? It would be easier to defend a Judas goat.

''Well, no. But I figured—''

''Forget it.''

''Look, I didn't mean to imply you'd sleep with a call girl, but who else would—''

''Leave it alone.''

''All I meant was, what kind of woman would—''

''I said, leave it alone, Cull.''

Keir and Cullen looked at each other again. Sean sat stiff and silent, trying to figure out why he'd almost made an ass of himself defending a woman who was not much better than Cull's description of her.

He was returning to Emeraude to deal with Alain Beaumont. It had nothing to do with Savannah. With the way she came to him in his dreams so that he'd lived that same moment a thousand times, her suddenly trembling in his arms, returning his kiss, sighing against his mouth…

"So," he said briskly, "Ma really does seem fine."

His brothers nodded, both of them grateful for the change in conversation.

"Absolutely." Cullen grinned. "Did you hear her chew out the nurse who insisted she had to leave the hospital in a wheelchair?"

The brothers chuckled, then took long pulls at their mugs of ale. Keir circled the wet rim of his glass with the tip of his index finger.

"That birthday party is gonna be some kind of event."

"Nice of the girls to offer to plan it," Sean said.

Cullen gave a dramatic shudder. "Whatever you do, don't let 'em catch you calling them 'girls.' Besides, 'nice' has nothing to do with it. They just don't trust Dan or us to get it right." He motioned to the waitress for another round. "Either of you have any idea what you're going to give Ma as a gift?"

"Cassie thought maybe a cruise to Hawaii."

"Marissa's thinking along the same lines. She suggested a week in Paris."

"Not bad. Hawaii this winter, Paris come summer… Sean? Want to toss in a spring vacation?"

Sean shifted uneasily in his seat. "I've got a problem with that."

"What? With giving her a trip?"

"With what to give Ma. She won't want a trip. Not from me."

"How do you know that?"

Sean took a few peanuts from the bowl and rolled them in his hand. "Idiot that I am, I asked her what she wanted."

"And?"

"And she told me."

Cullen and Keir looked at each other. "Well?" Cullen said. "You gonna keep us in suspense?"

"She wants..." Sean hesitated. Even now, it sounded impossible. "She said she wants me to get married."

There were a few seconds of silence. Then Keir laughed. "Trust Mary Elizabeth to get straight to the point."

"It's what she wants."

"Sure it is, but she'll settle for a trip to... What?"

Sean took a deep breath, then let it out. "I promised."

His brothers stared at him. "You what?"

"Don't look at me that way! How was I to know she'd ask for something so crazy?"

"Right. And Ma won't expect you to keep a crazy promise. She'll understand."

"Exactly. It's like when you're joking around and somebody says, you know what I'd really like? And you say tell me what it is and I'll do it, but both of you know it's just..." Cullen's words drifted to silence. "You really promised?"

"I really promised." Sean looked up. "I'd do anything for Ma. But this..."

"Do you even *know* a woman you'd want to marry?" Keir asked, and sighed with resignation when Sean laughed. "Well, you could always hire an actress."

"Yeah," Sean said glumly. "Too bad Greta Garbo's dead."

The brothers all chuckled. After a while, the topic turned to the latest baseball trade and everybody but Sean forgot all about it.

MA WON'T EXPECT you to keep a crazy promise. She'll understand.

Sean turned off the reading lamp above his seat in Trans Carib's first-class cabin. That was the trouble. His mother *would* understand. She'd look at him and sigh, and give that little smile that meant he'd failed her again.

He'd always failed her.

Cullen won every athletic award in high school. Keir won every academic honor. They'd both finished college, gone to grad school and made places for themselves in the world.

What had he ever done besides cause trouble?

He'd been suspended more times than he wanted to remember in high school, mostly because he hated sitting in a classroom. He'd loved hockey and he'd been good at it. Great, maybe, until the day a puck damned near took his eye out because he'd been a smart-ass who wouldn't wear a helmet with a visor. Yeah, he'd finished college but he'd floated through, all the time just yearning for graduation so he could bum around the world with a backpack.

Sean frowned at his reflection in the window.

That was then. This was now. He'd made a fortune. The backpack had turned into handmade leather luggage, he stayed in five-star hotels instead of hostels, and if he didn't have a permanent base, it was because he preferred it that way. He'd changed. He'd found success. He was the luckiest O'Connell brother. The one with nothing holding him down, nobody holding him back...

He was the brother who had nobody.

The universe seemed to hold its breath. A chasm, dark and deep, yawned at Sean's feet.

"Mr. O'Connell?" The flight attendant smiled. "Your dinner, sir."

"I'm not..." Sean hesitated, forced a smile. "Great. Thank you."

The girl set down his tray, poured his wine. Alone again, Sean ignored the filet mignon and reached for the burgundy. His mother's brush with death must have affected him more than he'd realized. Funny, how easily a man's perspective could get skewed.

He had everything. He was living a life he loved. Sean raised his glass and saw his reflection. Not everybody could say that, he thought, and suddenly, the face he saw in the glass wasn't his.

Savannah looked back at him.

Was scamming strangers a life she loved? Coming on to men to ensure a win? Did having Alain Beaumont put his hands on her make her happy?

What was with him tonight? What did he care what made Savannah McRae happy? How come he couldn't get it through his head that the tears she'd shed, the way she'd melted in his arms, had all been part of the act?

Sean tilted the glass to his lips and drank. He was going to stop thinking about Savannah. She didn't mean a thing to him. And he was going to take his brothers' advice and tell his mother the truth.

Ma, he'd say, *I never should have made you a promise I can't possibly keep.*

But before he did that, he'd confront Beaumont and his mistress. They owed him, and he was damned well going to collect.

IVORY MOONLIGHT dappled the dark waters of the Caribbean where the *Lorelei* lay at anchor. The night was warm and still. Savannah, alone in her stateroom, was counting the minutes until Alain left to go ashore.

Only then would she feel safe.

A tremor raced through her. Despite the heat, she felt

chilled. She reached for a sweatshirt and pulled it on over her thin cotton T-shirt.

Ten days had passed since the night she'd ruined everything. Ten days, but it felt like an eternity. Alain alternated between rage and deadly silence. Of the two, she'd begun to think his silence was the worst.

He was planning something. She knew it. He had been, ever since...

She had to stop thinking about that terrible night, but how could she? Alain was going to do something to punish her for what had happened. Wondering what and when was killing her.

It had taken her a very long time to get back to the harbor that night. She'd left the hotel by a back door, walked down the hill, then along the road. At dawn, an old man with a donkey cart gave her a lift. He hadn't asked her any questions. Maybe women with tear-stained faces, limping along in evening wear, were standard issue here.

The tender had been waiting at the dock; for one wild minute, she'd imagined turning around and running away. Then she'd thought of Missy, and she'd stepped into the boat and let the crewman take her to the *Lorelei*.

Alain was waiting in the yacht's salon, his face white, his mouth twisted into a narrow line. One look, and she knew he'd already heard the story.

Not all of it, of course. Not what had happened in O'Connell's bedroom, how the realization of what came next had suddenly become real.

All Alain knew was that she'd lost. It was enough.

"Alain," she'd said quickly, "I'm sorry. I did everything I could and it almost worked, but—"

He grabbed her so hard that she'd borne the marks of his fingers on her arms for days. Grabbed her and shaken her like a rag doll.

"You stupid *putain!*"

Even now, she shuddered, remembering the venom in his voice.

"How could you do this to me?" he'd roared.

"I told you," she whispered, "I don't know what happened. He was losing. And then—and then—"

Alain slapped her, hard enough to whip her head back. "Do you know what you cost me tonight?"

"Yes. Yes, I know. Almost five hundred thou—"

"Almost half a million dollars. How will you pay it back?"

"I'll win it at cards. I promise."

"How? By playing with my money? Does that sound reasonable to you?"

"It's—it's the best I can—"

"Shut up!" His spittle flew into her face as he leaned toward her. "Did you think I was joking? About wanting you to make O'Connell look like a fool?"

"No. No, of course not. But—"

"You didn't make a fool of him. He made a fool of you!"

"Alain, you must believe me. I was winning. I don't know what happened, only that suddenly—"

"When did you tell him you know me?"

"I never—"

"Don't lie to me! You told him. And that's who you made a fool of, you brainless creature. Me. Me! O'Connell's probably still laughing."

"No. He didn't laugh. Not at you!"

"I told you not to lie to me." Alain flung her from him. "And I told you the price you'd pay," he snarled and reached for the phone.

Missy. He was going to take Missy out of her safe haven in Switzerland. Savannah threw herself between him and the desk.

"I beg you, don't take this out on my sister."

"You failed me, Savannah. Apparently, your sister's welfare doesn't mean as much to you as I thought."

"Alain." Her voice trembled. She'd swallowed hard, fought for composure. "I'll win back the money. Every cent. I swear it."

His smile was the epitome of cruelty. "And will you win back your virginity? That's all you ever had, you know. Your skill at cards and your hymen." He thrust his face inches from hers. "And now they're both gone."

She started to tell him he was wrong, that she hadn't slept with Sean, but she caught herself just in time. That might make him only more furious, knowing she'd reneged on her wager. In the small world in which they lived, it meant she and anyone closely associated with her would be known as welshers.

Alain cursed, grabbed her arm, hustled her out of the salon and into her stateroom, slamming the door after her. Savannah had stood in the darkened cabin, shaking and shaken.

What he'd said, the way he'd said it... He'd made her virginity sound like a prize in a lottery. She wasn't surprised he knew she was innocent; when he'd first taken her from New Orleans, he'd demanded she undergo a complete physical examination.

"I'm entitled to know if there's any danger you carry disease," he'd said, and she'd burned with embarrassment even though the doctor had been brisk and professional.

But what did he mean, that all she'd ever had was her skill at cards and her virginity?

You know, a sly voice had seemed to whisper. It had to do with the way he'd taken to looking at her lately. The way he'd started talking about her with his friends. The way they'd turn their eyes on her, smile, all but lick their lips.

Savannah had shuddered. No. She wasn't going to think like that. Alain was just angry. He'd get over it.

But he hadn't. For ten days now, she'd been waiting for something to happen. Thus far, Alain had done nothing. He hadn't arranged any card games on his yacht, or sent her to play on shore. And he'd made a point of assuring her that Missy was still in her school.

The cabin door suddenly swung open, cutting short Savannah's musings. She swung around, saw Alain—and, for a moment, felt a weight lift from her shoulders. He didn't look angry. He didn't look threatening at all. He was dressed in a tux and, most surprising, he was smiling.

Then she realized it was the kind of smile that made the cabin seem suddenly airless. Savannah forced herself not to react. Whatever happened next, she wasn't going to give him the pleasure of hearing her beg.

"Good evening, *chérie*."

"Alain."

"You have half an hour to dress."

"Excuse me?"

"Is there a problem with your hearing, Savannah? I said you have half an hour to dress. Wear something long. Slinky. No, on second thought, put on something elegant." A smile lifted the corners of his lips. "It always amazes me that people think they know what's in a book by the look of the cover."

She almost sagged with relief. She'd read him wrong. Everything was okay. Alain was going to take her to the casino, or perhaps to one of the island's mansions. She didn't care where he took her. What counted was that he was going to let her play for him again and win back the money she'd lost.

"Thank you, Alain. You won't regret it. Where are we going? I'll win a lot of money, more than I lost, and—"

"We're not going ashore." He shot back his cuff and checked his watch. "I'm expecting guests in a little while. Forty minutes, to be exact, but, of course, I want to see how you look before they arrive."

"Alain," she called as he swung away from her. "Wait." He looked at her, eyebrows raised, and she forced a smile. "Who am I going to play?"

"Play?" He chuckled. "I can't see that it will matter to you."

"You know that it does. You can tell me the weaknesses of the other players."

"Ah." He nodded solemnly and tucked his hands into his trouser pockets. "I'm afraid you misunderstood, *chérie*. You see, I've a plan that will enable you to repay me the money you lost."

"Yes. I realize that. And I promise, I'll play well. It shouldn't take too long."

"To win back the money?" He smiled, rocked back on his heels. "No, it probably won't. Now that I've had time to think things over, I'm willing to admit you're still worth something to me."

She nodded. Her mouth was dry with relief. She'd be playing again. Winning again. With all this time on her hands, she'd thought of a couple of ways she might be able to skim a little money. It would be dangerous, and it would take a very long time, but if she were careful, if she were lucky, she might be able to put together enough to see her through a few months of Missy's care while she found a job to support them both.

Just thinking about the future made it easy to smile.

"Thank you, Alain. You won't regret this. I lost to Sean O'Connell, but I'm still one of the best card—"

"I told you, that's not at issue. In fact, I don't want you to win."

She stared at him. "You don't? But if I don't win, how can I pay back what I owe you?"

"Darling girl, I'd expect more creativity from a street hustler! Why would you think there's only one way to repay your debt? You have other talents besides playing cards, Savannah. Many of my friends have noticed. And *I've* noticed that many of *them* lead dull lives. I've come up with a way to combine their appreciation of you with their desire to lead more interesting existences, *chérie*. Isn't that clever of me?"

A chill speared through her blood.

"Well," she said, forcing a little smile, "your friends always seem to enjoy playing poker here. The *Lorelei* is—"

"Most of them own yachts of their own," he said with a dismissive gesture. "Charming as *Lorelei* may be, she's nothing new to them."

"I don't—I don't—"

The sound of the tender's engine interrupted her words. Alain tut-tutted and checked his watch again.

"Our first guests. They're early but it's understandable. Who wouldn't be eager to play our new game?"

Savannah felt her legs giving out. She couldn't show weakness. Not now.

"I don't understand what you're suggesting, Alain."

"It's quite simple, *chérie*. I've devised an entertainment, something a bit unusual. It will be far more profitable than if you were simply to play against them and win."

Slowly, he reached out and ran his hand down her cheek. Savannah flinched. That won her an oily grin.

"Come on, darling, don't play dumb. The streets of New Orleans schooled you well, *non?* I'll provide the players. You'll provide the incentive. Why do you still look puzzled, Savannah? It's a simple plan. We're going to hold a poker elimination tournament. Several, to be precise, until the novelty fades. A timed game each weekday night, with the biggest winners to play against each other on Saturdays." He flashed another smile, bigger than the last. "The stakes will be very, very high, *chérie*. High enough to be worthy of you."

"Worthy of me?" Savannah said in a small voice.

"Certainly." Alain grinned. "Don't you see? The final winner wins you!"

Savannah felt the blood drain from her head. "Are you crazy?"

"I admit, your value might be a bit greater if you were still, as we say, intact, but look at the amount O'Connell was willing to wager without even realizing you were a virgin." He chuckled. "I suppose I should thank him, should I ever have the misfortune to see him again. After all, this is his idea, when you come down to it, and it's brilliant."

She stared at him, struggling for words that wouldn't come. Her heart, her breath, seemed to have stopped.

"Alain," she said, trying to sound calm, "this isn't funny."

"It isn't meant to be." Alain tucked his hands in the pockets of his trousers and rocked back on his heels. "Life can get so dull, *chérie*. I should think you'd applaud my efforts to brighten it."

"I'm not a whore!"

His false smile vanished. "You'll be whatever I tell you to be."

"No. No!"

"After all I've done for you and that pathetic sister of yours, I finally asked one thing in return. 'Humiliate Sean O'Connell,' I said. And you didn't do it."

"I tried. I'm sorry it went wrong, but—"

"There are no 'buts,' Savannah. Failure is failure. All

things considered, I think I'm going out of my way to be generous. After I deduct the money you owe me and expenses, there'll be a tidy sum left. It will be yours.''

Bile rose in her throat. "I won't do it!''

Alain's false good humor vanished. He caught hold of Savannah's wrist. "Yes, you will.''

"You're insane!''

"The lady's right, Beaumont,'' a deep, lazy voice said. "You always were a crazy son of a bitch.''

Alain let go of Savannah and spun toward the door. Savannah caught her breath.

"Sean?'' she whispered. "Oh God, Sean!''

Sean dragged his eyes from Beaumont long enough to look at Savannah. Her face was white; her eyes were enormous, but when she saw him they began to shine. Her mouth trembled, then lifted in a smile.

She made him feel as if he were mounted on that prancing white horse.

For one heart-stopping minute, he wanted to go to her, sweep her into his arms and tell her he'd protect her. Then he remembered what he'd overheard. It looked as if he'd walked in on a lovers' quarrel about money.

His gut knotted. He'd been a fool to let Savannah haunt his dreams and not to have taken her when he could. She wasn't even a call girl, as Cullen had implied. That was too high-class a term.

"O'Connell?'' Alain's voice was strained. "How did you get on this boat?''

Sean turned his attention to Beaumont. "Why, you were kind enough to send your tender for me,'' he said softly. "I thought that was a mighty decent gesture.''

"You lied your way onto this vessel!'' Beaumont grabbed the intercom. "I'll have you thrown overboard. I'll have you—''

The words became a cry of pain as Sean caught his hand and bent it back. The intercom slid from Beaumont's grasp and he sank slowly to his knees.

"You're hurting me," he gasped.

"I want my money."

"What money? I don't know what—"

"Your lady friend played against me ten days ago. She lost."

"You just said, *she* played you. What has that to do with me?"

"Give me a break, Beaumont. She played for you."

Beads of sweat popped on Beaumont's forehead. "So what? She paid her debt."

"She didn't."

"What do you mean, she didn't? You won her for the night."

"Yeah, and I didn't collect."

Beaumont shot a look at Savannah. "What does he mean?"

"Nothing. Of course he collected, Alain. It's just—it's just that he wants more. Isn't that right, Mr. O'Connell?"

She turned away from Beaumont and stared at Sean. Her eyes, even her body language, implored him to go along with her lie. But why would he? He owed this woman nothing.

"Please," she mouthed silently.

"Yeah," Sean growled, mentally cursing himself for being a fool, "that's right. So I'm going to let you make up for it, Beaumont. I want a million bucks."

Beaumont turned whiter than he already was. "Why would I give you a million dollars?"

"Lots of reasons, starting with the fact that you wouldn't want me to spread the word that you're not only a liar, you're a man who sends a woman to seek a revenge he's too cowardly to attempt himself.'' Sean's smile had a savage edge. "Then there's the little matter of the lies you've spread about me. I've heard the rumors. You said I cheated you last summer when the truth is that you couldn't admit you'd lost.''

"Alain?'' Savannah whispered. "Is that true?''

"Your lover boy wouldn't know the truth if it bit him in the butt.'' Sean tightened his grip on Beaumont. "A million bucks, and I'm out of here.''

"Even if I wanted to give you that much, I couldn't. Ahh! You're breaking my wrist, O'Connell. Let go!''

"Let him go. Please.''

Sean flashed a look at Savannah. She looked desperate. Was there a heart somewhere inside her, and if so, did she really feel something for this pig?

The possibility made Sean's jaw clench. What in hell did it matter to him? Savannah McRae could have the hots for King Kong for all he gave a damn. Still, he was tired of listening to Beaumont whimper. Abruptly, he let go of the man's pudgy hand.

"Get up.''

Beaumont dragged himself to his feet as if he were dying and cupped his hand against his chest.

"You're almost as good an actor as your lady friend.''

"I think you broke a bone.''

"No such luck. Come on, Beaumont. I know your safe is in the salon. Take me to it, get me what you owe me and I'm gone.''

"I don't have that much money here. If you wait until Monday…''

Sean laughed. Beaumont swallowed hard.

"My marker is good everywhere.''

"Maybe, but not with me. I want cash.''

Braver now that Sean had let him get to his feet, Beaumont's mouth thinned. "I could charge you with theft."

"No, you couldn't." Sean jerked his chin at Savannah. "I have a witness who'll say otherwise."

"She'll say what I tell her to say. Won't you, *chérie?*" Savannah didn't answer. Beaumont narrowed his eyes. "Won't you?" he said in a menacing whisper.

He raised his hand. Sean moved quickly, grabbed him and threw him against the wall.

"Don't touch her," he growled.

"She's mine. I created her and I'll do whatever I like to her."

A soft cry burst from Savannah's throat. Sean watched as she buried her face in her hands. Her hair, loose as it had been that night, tumbled around her face…but it wasn't as it had been that night. Not really. Then, it had been combed into artful disorder. Now, it hung in curls that were wild and real.

Everything about her was different from the last time. She wore no makeup, no jewels. No do-me heels and sexy dress. Instead, she had on a baggy sweatshirt, faded, loose jeans and sneakers.

She looked vulnerable. Beautiful. Sweet and innocent, the kind of woman a man would give his soul to possess.

The kind a man could take home to his mother.

Sean blinked. Beaumont chuckled. "Ahhh," he breathed.

Sean's eyes flashed to his face. Beaumont had gone from looking as if the world were about to end to smiling, if you wanted to call the smirk on his fleshy lips a smile.

"Ah, what? Did you just remember that you have enough money in your safe?"

"No, Mr. O'Connell. I just thought of what I can offer you to satisfy your demand."

"I'm not in the market for a yacht, Beaumont."

"How about a woman? Are you in the market for that?"

"No!" Savannah shook her head wildly. "Alain. You can't. I won't. I swear, if you try to do this, I'll—"

"This woman owes me five hundred thousand dollars. And you just said you came here because you want more of her. Well, you can have her," Beaumont said, jerking his chin at Savannah. "For... Let's see. A week?"

"Alain. Please, Alain..."

"Not enough? How about two weeks?" A smile crawled across his mouth. "Surely you can think of something to do with a woman like Savannah for fourteen days and nights."

Sean saw a blur of motion out of the corner of his eye, and then Savannah was on Beaumont, clawing at him while he staggered and tried to protect his face.

"I'll kill you," she panted. "I swear, I'll—"

Sean grabbed her, pulled her back against him and pinned her in place with an arm wrapped tightly around her waist. His hand lay just under her breast; he could feel her heart beating against his palm.

Once, decades before, he'd felt a heart beating that same way.

He'd been eight, maybe nine; he'd been in big trouble at home for playing hooky and had gone to a hidey-hole he knew in a lot behind the Desert Song. That day, his hiding place already had an occupant. A tiny songbird lay on its back, beak open as it panted for breath.

He knew something terrible had happened to the bird and he wanted to help it, but he couldn't. All he could do was cradle it in his hand and feel the terrified gallop of its heart.

"Well, O'Connell? Yes or no?"

To hell with that long-ago wounded bird. He had an opportunity here that could solve his problem.

"The woman," Sean said. "For two weeks."

"No," Savannah moaned, but Beaumont nodded his head and the deal was done.

CHAPTER EIGHT

SAVANNAH DIDN'T GO QUIETLY.

She shrieked, raged, yelled that she wasn't property, but Sean encircled her wrist with a hand that felt like a manacle and propelled her up the ladder to the deck.

"Move," he said through clenched teeth, "or I'll toss you over my shoulder and carry you off this damned boat."

Had she really felt her heart lift with hope when she first saw O'Connell in the doorway? She was a fool to have expected anything good from a man with his morals. So what if he'd won her that night and not taken her to bed? That wasn't enough to mark him as her savior. Whatever the reason he hadn't demanded full payment, he was going to demand it now.

He could demand what he liked, but she'd be damned if he'd get it without a fight.

Savannah slammed her elbow into his belly. He grunted at the force of the blow.

"You stupid son of a bitch," she panted. "Do you really think you can get away with this? Let go or I'll report you to the police."

"You'd have to get past your boyfriend first." Sean dragged her to where a ladder led down to the tender. "Somehow, I don't think he'd let that happen. Besides, what would you tell the cops?" She balked when they reached the ladder and he pushed her forward. "I can get fifty witnesses to tell them how you handed yourself over to me a couple of weeks ago at the casino."

"That has nothing to do with what you're doing now."

"Sure it does. We're just picking up where we left off. Get down that ladder."

"I won't!"

Savannah jammed her feet against the teak deck coaming. Sean cursed and slung her over his shoulder, just as he'd threatened. She roared with frustration and pounded her fists against his back. The ladder swayed precariously under his feet.

"You want to go for a swim, babe? Keep that up and, so help me, I'll dump you in the drink."

She believed him. He was a man of zero principles. Maybe Alain had lied about him cheating in that card game. Maybe he hadn't. A man who'd accept a woman in payment and carry her off was capable of anything.

"Alain lied," she said desperately, as he dropped her into a seat in the tender. "He keeps a lot of money in his safe."

Sean folded his arms and spread his feet apart.

"And you'd know all about his money."

"A million, at least," she said, refusing to be drawn away from the topic. "You could tell him you changed your mind. That you want money, not—not—"

Sean smiled coldly. "But I haven't changed my mind. I have exactly what I came for."

Her face flooded with color. "Is that the kind of man you are, O'Connell? Do you buy your women?"

"You're the one who put yourself up for sale, sugar."

"That's not true! You were the one who suggested I make that wager that night."

"And you leaped at it like a dog at a bone. Besides, what would Beaumont say if I told him I was bringing you back because you were uncooperative? According to you, I came back for more of what I already got." He smiled thinly. "I don't think he'd be very happy but hey, what do I know? Maybe I don't understand the complexity of the relationship."

The threat seemed to work. He could almost see the fight going out of her. Her head drooped forward; her hair tumbled around her face. Seeing her like this, her posture one of defeat, put a hollow feeling in Sean's belly. She was a liar. A cheat. A better con artist than any he'd ever met, and that was saying a lot.

But he could make things easier. All he had to do was tell her the truth, that Beaumont had triggered an idea and it had nothing to do with sex.

"What's wrong, sugar? It's just another slice off the loaf."

Savannah's head came up. She opened her mouth, on the verge of telling him she had never slept with Alain or anyone else, but why bother? He wouldn't believe her. More to the point, why defend herself to a man like this?

He was right. She really didn't have any choice. She'd cost Alain a fortune. Worse, she'd cost him his pride. He was demanding payback and he held her sister's well-being in the palm of his hand. If she refused to do his bidding, Missy would pay for it.

"You're right," she said wearily. "What does it matter which of you I'm with? You're both snakes in the same pit."

Her words jolted Sean. It wasn't true. Beaumont had used this woman in a scheme of revenge, but he...he—

Her head was down again, her face made invisible by her hair. When she raised a hand and brushed at her eyes, he knew she was crying.

Hell. The truth was, he was going to use her, too, and he suspected that even an ethicist would have a tough time making it sound as if his using her to live a lie was better than Beaumont using her in a petty game of get-even.

But he wasn't Beaumont, damn it. Not that it mattered what she thought of him, but he wanted her to know that.

"Maybe it's true," he said gruffly. "Maybe there isn't a lot of difference between him and me—except for one thing."

Savannah looked up. He'd judged correctly. Tears glittered on her lashes and he fought the desire to take her in his arms and brush them away, until he recalled how she'd pulled that same stunt the last time.

"I don't believe in owning people, Savannah."

She gave a watery laugh. Sean stood straighter.

"You behave yourself, do as you're told, give the kind of performance I expect, and I'll pay you."

Her face turned white at the word "performance." He was about to explain what he'd meant but before he could, she drew a deep breath and expelled it. When she looked at him again, her eyes were flat.

"How much?"

Her voice was low. So low that he had to lean forward to make sure he'd heard the question. It staggered him. Was it that simple? Mention money, and she turned docile as a lamb?

It shouldn't have come as a surprise. He knew exactly what she was. The tears, tonight's sweetly girlish looks didn't mean a thing. They were window dressing laid over the skeleton of what Savannah McRae really was.

"How much?" she said again, her voice a little stronger.

Sean clenched his jaw. "Don't you want to know what you're going to be required to do first?"

Color swept into her cheeks. "I'm not stupid, O'Connell. You don't have to spell it out."

He thought of telling her she was wrong, but he'd be

damned if he was going to tell her anything more than he had to. What she did didn't matter to her. Only money was important.

Besides, she'd never believe him. What would he say? *I want you to pretend to be my fiancée?* He was having a bad enough time believing it himself. What had ever possessed him to come up with such an impossible scheme? Why hadn't he taken the time to think it over?

Then again, why would he? Life on the edge had always been his thing.

He swung away, snapped "Shove off" to the crewman. The engine started and the tender leaped forward. The roar of the motor and the slap of the sea against the hull provided enough of a sound block so the guy driving the boat wouldn't hear what he said next.

"What's the most you've ever won in a poker game?"

She gave him a chilly smile. "Women and cards. Yours is a simple world, O'Connell."

"Sleeping with Beaumont and scamming strangers," Sean said coldly. "Anybody can see that your world is far more intricate than mine."

Her eyes filled with heat. She wanted to fly at him as she had earlier; he saw it in her face. Hell, he wanted her to. Wanted to hold her against him, subdue her, kiss her until she moaned...

"Answer the question," he snapped, his anger at himself almost as great as his anger at her.

"Four hundred thousand," she said, lifting her chin in defiance. "That was my record. I'd have topped it by a hundred thou if I'd won the night I played you."

"But you didn't."

"I came close."

"Only because I let you."

"Am I supposed to apologize for that? Poker's as much a game of tactics as it is chance."

The lady gave as good as she got. That was probably her only redeeming quality.

"What you mean is, it helps to be a good actor." The wind ruffled Sean's hair. He pushed it back from his forehead. "It's why I wanted you."

Color filled her face again. Sean almost laughed.

"Forget that. I don't want you for anything kinky."

Nothing kinky, but he wanted her to act when he made love to her? She hated him. Despised him almost as much as she despised Alain.

"Five hundred thousand, Savannah. Exactly the amount I won from you." Sean smiled with his teeth. "That's what I'll pay you, if I'm satisfied with the job you do."

Her mouth fell open. For a second, she looked as if she were going to leap up and dance him in wild circles. His gut knotted with distaste. Half a million bucks could go a long way toward making a woman like this happy.

Then she seemed to get herself under control. "Those terms are acceptable."

She spoke without emotion. For the second time in minutes, he wanted to take her in his arms, not to comfort her but to shake her.

I just bought you, he wanted to snarl. *I can use you anyway I want. Doesn't that bother you?*

Evidently not.

"Done," he said, and held out his hand as the tender bumped against the dock.

O'CONNELL HERDED HER into his car. Then he took out his cell phone. She didn't pay much attention to his conversation, which seemed to consist mostly of commands.

He had a command for her, too. "Buckle up."

She'd already done that. The memory of his hand slipping across her breasts was still vivid. He'd touch her soon enough, but she wasn't going to offer up an opportunity.

Savannah shuddered. Think about something else, she told herself. Fortunately, O'Connell made it easy to do.

The man drove like a maniac.

He was in a hurry to get to his hotel. Things had not gone as he'd hoped the last time he'd brought her to his bedroom. This time would be different.

She'd given her promise.

It was too late for regrets. Agreeing to O'Connell's offer had been her only choice. Now, all she could do was hope. That he wouldn't hurt her. That he wouldn't force things on her.

She knew some of what could happen when a rich, powerful man thought he owned a woman. The men who played cards on the yacht sometimes brought women with then. She'd overhead things.

Savannah shuddered again. Two weeks, that was all. Surely, she could endure whatever he did to her for that long. He was handsome. Not that it mattered but at least she wouldn't have to gag whenever he came near her.

She knew that there were woman who'd envy her.

A woman wouldn't have to act if this man took her to bed. She'd go willingly. Eagerly. She'd sigh when he put his hands on her, moan when he teased her lips apart with his.

She shut her eyes and thought back to that first time he'd taken her to his hotel. He could have done anything he wanted. And he'd wanted, all right. There'd been no mistaking the hardness of his arousal when he'd gathered her into his arms, but she'd wept and he'd sent her away. Yes, he'd been furious and, yes, he'd humiliated her by tossing money at her feet, but he hadn't done what he'd been entitled to do.

He'd done enough, though. Touched her. Kissed her. Sometimes, in the deepest part of the night, she thought she could still feel his hands on her, his mouth...

Savannah sat up straight.

What did any of that matter? She'd made a deal with Sean O'Connell and if she kept her part of it and he kept his, she'd have the money it would take to fly to Switzerland and take Missy to a new place where she'd get the same excellent treatment. She'd cover their trail carefully so Alain could never find them.

She had to keep all that in mind. It would make what came next bearable.

The car purred as Sean downshifted. Savannah blinked and focused on the blur of palms, white sand and blue water outside the window. Had they sped past the turnoff to his hotel? Yes. Yes, they had. A town called *Bijou* lay ahead of them. It was reputed to live up to its name by being a jewel box of designer and couturier boutiques, all in keeping with Emeraude's profile as an unspoiled playground for the incredibly rich.

Why was O'Connell taking her there?

"We're going to do some shopping," he said, as if she'd spoken the question aloud.

Shopping? In *Bijou?*

"If you'd given me time to pack, you wouldn't have to buy me a toothbrush."

She tried to sound flippant. It didn't work. Her voice was scratchy and it shook. Damn it, she wasn't going to let him see her sweat. What kind of shopping did he have in mind? Leather? Teenybopper minis? A froth of lace that would turn her into an obscene version of an upstairs maid? Maybe the shops here carried such things. From what she'd observed of Alain's friends, the very rich could also be very decadent.

O'Connell slowed the car as they entered the town. Under other circumstances, she'd have been enthralled. Cobblestone streets radiated from a central fountain surrounded by lush beds of bougainvillea. Mercedes, Ferraris, Maseratis and Lamborghinis were neatly parked along the curbs.

How did they get all those cars to this dot in the ocean? Savannah thought, and almost laughed aloud at the absurdity of the question. The rich and powerful could arrange for anything. Wasn't her presence at O'Connell's side proof of that?

He pulled into a parking space, got out of the car, came around to her side. "Out," he said, pulling open the door.

She got out. It was late—almost nine—and the shops were shuttered. So much for O'Connell's shopping trip, she thought, but he took her arm and tugged her toward the nearest door.

No leather in the windows. No cheesy minis or endless yards of lace, either. There was nothing in the windows except discreet gold script that spelled out a name so well-known it seemed to ooze money.

"They're closed," she said, and came to a halt.

"They're open. I phoned when we left the harbor."

So that was what the commands had been all about. O'Connell could get a place like this to stay open for him?

"How'd you pull that off?" she said pleasantly. "Is the manager into you for a gambling debt?"

"You've got a smart mouth, McRae." Sean's hand tightened on her elbow. "Let's go."

"I don't know what you're thinking," Savannah said quickly, "but I promise you, I am not spending a penny of what you're going to pay me on anything this place sells."

He turned toward her. She saw a muscle knot in his jaw.

"Is that your deal with Beaumont? Does he give you money, then make you pay for your clothing out of it?"

Alain bought her clothes. Not jeans or shorts or the cotton tops she lived in. She ordered those online, paid for them with the small amount of money he permitted her to keep from her gambling winnings. He bought her gowns and the accessories to go with them. His taste had never been hers but lately, it made her stomach turn. He'd begun buying her things that made her feel cheap.

"You're a beautiful woman, *chérie*," he said when she protested a dress cut too low, a gown with too high a slit. "Why hide it from the world?"

But there wasn't a reason in hell to tell any of that to this man.

"My arrangements with Alain have nothing to do with you," she said coolly. "I'm talking about our deal, O'Connell."

"Relax, sugar. I have no intention of making you pay. In our little drama, wardrobe's the director's responsibility."

"Just what is our little drama? I think I'm entitled to know."

He bent his head to hers. "You're my fiancée."

"Excuse me?"

"You heard me," he said with impatience. "For the next two weeks, you're my fiancée. We're here to buy you whatever you'll need to return to the States with me and meet my family."

Savannah stared at him. So much for leather and upstairs maids. "*That's* your fantasy?"

His laugh was quick and harsh. "Believe me," he said, "it's damned near as much a surprise to me as it is to you."

He put his hand into the small of her back and opened the door. A bell tinkled discreetly somewhere in the distance as they stepped into a hushed world of ivory silk, mirrored walls and low couches. The elusive scent of expensive perfume drifted on the air.

A salesclerk, dressed in the same ivory silk that paneled the walls and covered the couches, glided toward them.

"Wait," Savannah said frantically. "What assurance do I have that you'll keep your end of our bargain?"

The cold look O'Connell gave her almost stopped her heart. He held up his hand. The clerk smiled and stayed where she was.

"The same assurance I have that you'll keep yours," he said in a low voice. "My word."

She thought about telling him his word didn't mean much, but that would have been a lie. A gambler's word was everything.

"You don't want to accept it, we can call the whole thing off. I'll take you back to the *Lorelei.* You can explain your return to Beaumont."

Savannah shook her head. "Your word is good enough."

"And yours?"

Their eyes met. He'd slipped his arm around her waist; he was holding her against him, a little smile playing on his mouth. She knew it was in preparation for the charade they were about to perform for the clerk but for a moment, oh, just for a moment, she imagined what it would be like if he were taking her to this place because she mattered to him, because he wanted to see her in silks and cashmeres, wanted to enjoy the sight of her in them in public, the excitement of stripping them from her when they were alone.

A tremor went through her, and she blanked the ridiculous images from her mind.

"My word's as good as yours, O'Connell."

"Sean."

"Does it matter?"

"Yes. My fiancée would call me by my first name."

"You want to explain what this is all about?"

His lips twisted. "In due time." His gaze dropped to her mouth. "But first—first, I think we need to formalize our arrangement."

"Formalize it?"

"Uh-huh." He looked into her eyes. What she saw in his—the heat, the hunger—made her breath catch. "Something in lieu of signing a contract in front of a notary public."

Slowly, he lowered his mouth to hers. From the corner of her eye, she saw the clerk turn discreetly away. There was no question what he was going to do. And there was time, plenty of time, to draw back or at least to turn her head to the side. Savannah did neither. She would let him kiss her. Wasn't the kiss part of what she'd agreed to?

She'd let it happen solely for that.

Still, when his mouth touched hers, she felt her knees buckle. He drew her closer, kissed her again. The blood roared in her ears and she moaned softly against his lips. Her heart began to pound. She knew that his was, too. She could feel it galloping against hers.

Sean drew back, his hands cupping her shoulders, holding her away from him. Savannah opened her eyes. His expression was shuttered and cold.

"My fiancée is ready now," he said.

The words were directed to the clerk, but they might as well have been for her. His message was clear. He could turn her on anytime he wanted. He knew it. Now, she knew it, too.

The realization made her feel cheaper than she already did.

Really, she hadn't thought that was possible.

CHAPTER NINE

THEY WERE STILL CHOOSING clothes and accessories as midnight approached.

At least, Sean was. Savannah was simply a mannequin standing before him on a little platform in front of a wall of mirrors.

At first, he didn't even bother asking her opinion. The clerk would bring out an armful of clothing and display it.

Yes, he'd say, *no, yes, maybe.*

Then the clerk would take Savannah to the fitting room where she'd put on the dress or suit or whatever Sean had chosen, slip into matching shoes the clerk seemed to whisk out of the air, and go out to the platform to await a nod of approval.

After a while, Sean began asking what she thought.

"Do you like this?" he'd say, and she'd look into the glass, at the stranger looking back, a woman with her eyes, her face, her body.

Where was the girl who'd worn clothes salvaged from thrift shop donation bins? The supposed sophisticate whose clothes were chosen by Alain? What had become of the con artist dressed in red silk?

Sean was turning her into someone she'd never been. Or maybe someone she'd always wanted to be.

Yes, she wanted to say, *oh, yes, I like it. I like it a lot.*

But she didn't because this wasn't real and he didn't actually care if she liked something or not. He was just getting tired or maybe bored. Maybe both. So she shrugged her shoulders and said yes, sure, the outfit was okay.

"We'll take it," Sean would say.

By then, the clerk had lost her laid-back façade. She looked like someone who'd won the lottery. Even her French accent started slipping, and when Sean approved a long column of white silk that had to cost the earth, moon and stars, the accent disappeared altogether in a rush of pure New York.

"Doesn't the lady look *gawjiss?*" the clerk babbled. A rush of bright pink flooded her face. "I mean—I mean, *madame* is so chic!"

Savannah laughed. It was an unlikely thing to do, considering the circumstances and her state of mind, and she buried the burst of laughter in a cough. She fooled the clerk but one look in the mirror and she knew she hadn't fooled Sean. He was grinning like the Cheshire cat. Without thinking, she grinned back.

What a great smile he had. Lazy. Open. And yes, sexy enough to make her breath catch. Had he done this before? Taken a woman on a shopping spree? Bought her things that made her feel beautiful. Looked at her as if—as if—

Savannah tore her gaze from his. What did it matter? Sean was a smart, hard-as-nails gambler. His charm, when he chose to use it, was as much a lie as the easy smile.

How could she have come so close to forgetting that?

This wasn't a shopping spree, it was a step in some complex game he'd devised. He was remaking her. Did he have a thing about only bedding women whose appearance was genteel? Maybe that was why he'd sent her packing the night he'd won her. Maybe the red dress, the heels, had backfired, turning him off as much as they'd turned him on.

A wave of exhaustion shot through her, so intense and unexpected it rocked her back on her heels. She swayed and would have fallen if Sean hadn't already been at her side, enfolding her in his arms.

"Savannah?"

He turned her to him, said her name again. She wanted to tell him to let her go but she didn't. Just for this moment, she let herself lean against him and take strength from the feel of his body.

"What's wrong?"

She licked her dry lips. "Nothing."

"Try another answer." He cupped her chin in one hand and raised her face to his. "Are you ill?"

She shook her head. "I told you, I'm okay."

"Savannah." He bent his knees and peered into her face. "Hell," he said roughly, "you're white as a sheet."

His eyes were the palest blue she'd ever seen, and they weren't cold with anger or mockery as they had been that first time in his hotel room. He had a small scar on the bridge of his nose, another that feathered out delicately from his eyebrow, and she wondered how he'd gotten them, if they'd hurt, if anyone had soothed them with a touch.

"Savannah? What's the matter?"

She shook her head. His voice was soft. For some reason, the sound of it made her throat tighten. He was right, something *was* the matter, but how could she give him an answer when she didn't know it herself?

"I'm just—I'm tired," she said, "that's all."

His eyes narrowed. She expected them to flash with those familiar angry sparks but before she could read anything in their depths, he swept her up into his arms.

"Pack up everything and send it to me at the hotel Petite Fleur first thing in the morning," he told the astonished clerk.

"Everything, *monsieur?*"

"You heard me. Toss in whatever else my—my fiancée might need. Lingerie, purses, shoes... You figure it out."

Sean let the woman dance ahead of him to open the door. He stepped out into the dark night, *bon soirs* and *mercis* flying after him like a flock of nightingales.

"Really, O'Connell," Savannah said. "I can walk."

Her breath was warm against his throat. Her hair tickled his cheek. Holding her like this, he became aware of her scent, something that reminded him of summer flowers and misting rain.

"O'Connell..."

"I'll put you down as soon as we get to the... Here we are." He let her down gently, held her close against him while he opened the door to his car. Her hair brushed lightly against his face again as he eased her inside. He shut his eyes and concentrated on the silky glide of it against his skin. She turned her face; for an instant, their lips were a sigh apart and then she jerked back and he straightened so quickly he slammed his head on the roof. "Damn," he said, hissing with pain.

Savannah made a little move, as if she were going to touch him. Obviously, he was mistaken because when she spoke, her voice was cool.

"Sorry," she said, without sounding sorry at all. "You should have let me walk."

He'd tried to do something decent and what did he get for it? A contemptuous retort and a rap on the skull. So much for being a nice guy. Still, part of him knew he was overreacting. Not that it stopped him.

"You're right," he said as he went around the car and slipped behind the wheel, "but for a couple of minutes there, you looked as if you were going to collapse." He checked for traffic, found none, and shot away from the curb. "I can't afford to let my investment get damaged."

"No. Certainly not." There was a beat of silence. "Do you think you could let me know what's going on anytime soon?"

"When I'm good and ready."

"No problem. Have it your way."

Sean glanced at her. Her hands were locked together in her lap, her profile was stony and her words had been tossed off with a lack of care, but she didn't fool him. She was nervous. Well, why wouldn't she be? Whatever he thought of her morals or her lack of them, not knowing what she was getting into had to be disturbing.

He checked the mirror and stepped down on the gas pedal. The car gave a throaty roar and sped up the narrow coast road.

"I need you to put on a performance."

"I'm not stupid, O'Connell."

"Sean," he said through his teeth.

"All those clothes... The question is, who am I performing for? What role am I expected to play? And why? Unless you're one of those men who needs a fantasy to get it on."

Her voice quavered on the last few words, but the disdain was still there. He thought about jamming on the brakes, pulling her into his arms and showing her how little he needed fantasy or anything else as a turn-on, but he wasn't stupid, either.

The unvarnished truth was, she excited him.

It was one of the reasons he'd forgotten the lateness of the hour or that he hadn't so much as bought either of them a cup of coffee. At first, he'd told himself he just wanted to get this whole thing going before he came to his senses and asked himself what, exactly, he thought he was doing.

Halfway into the fashion parade, he'd known it was because he was too busy looking at Savannah to want to do anything else.

It wasn't the clothes. She looked beautiful in everything the clerk brought out, but he'd seen a lot of beautiful women in a lot of beautiful stuff over the years. He was beyond that as a turn-on.

What he'd gotten caught up in was watching her face in the mirror, how she'd gone from wariness to acceptance to surprised joy. It made him remember the time he'd sat in on a fashion shoot of his sister, Fallon. Her expression had gone through similar changes and she'd explained that it was part of the feature they were shooting.

I'm supposed to be a plain Jane, she'd told him, *transformed into a ravishing beauty by this designer's things.*

His sister was one fine model and the camera had captured her pleasure at the transformation but then, the magazine had been paying her something like ten thousand bucks for the morning's work.

He wasn't naive. Savannah was getting paid, too. Fifty times his sister's fee, but she hadn't looked half as happy when he'd offered her the money as she had the last couple of hours, just staring into the mirror. Something was happening within her. She was coming out of her chrysalis, watching herself change, and she liked what she saw.

So did he.

Then, minutes ago, she'd giggled. Giggled, as if she and the world were both innocent. And when he smiled at her in the mirror, she'd smiled back. Really smiled, the way a woman would smile at a man who was making her happy.

Sean's mouth turned down.

Damned right, he was making her happy. He'd promised her a half-million dollar payoff and now he was buying her more clothes than she'd ever need for what would ultimately be a couple of days' charade. What she'd been looking at, in that mirror, was one extremely fortunate female.

"Well?"

He looked across the console. Savannah was looking at him, her chin up, her arms folded over her seat belt. She was waiting for an answer and no matter what he thought of her, he figured it was time she got one.

"I come from a very close-knit family."

Her lips turned up at the corners. "How nice for you."

Sean gritted his teeth. Her tone made it clear she didn't give a damn if he came from a close family or from a den of serpents, but he couldn't see any sense in giving her less of an answer than she'd need to understand the part he expected her to play.

"I have two brothers and three sisters."

She yawned. "I'm thrilled."

"Two of my sisters are married. So are my two brothers."

"Listen, O'Conn... Listen, Sean, this is all very interesting if you're into family, but I'm not. How about getting to the bottom line?"

"My mother had a stroke a couple of weeks ago."

"Oh." Savannah swung toward him. "Did she...? I'm sorry."

Maybe she was. She sounded it. Not that he gave a damn. An actress didn't have to believe in a role, she just had to play it.

"She came though it with flying colors." He grinned; he couldn't help it. Just thinking about his mother's feistiness made him smile. Mary Elizabeth would like Savannah, he thought suddenly. She'd admire her toughness. Her resiliency...and what in hell did that have to do with anything?

He frowned and cleared his throat. "But for a while there, we thought she wasn't going to make it. And afterward—afterward, I asked her what she wanted for her birthday." He gave a little laugh. "I said I'd give it to her, no matter what it was."

"That was nice."

Savannah's voice was low. He glanced at her. She sounded as if she might be smiling, but it was too dark to see her face.

"Yeah. I mean, it was supposed to be, but she caught me by surprise when she told me what it was."

She laughed, the same way she had in the dress shop. The sound was so sweet that it made him smile, too.

"Let me guess. She wanted an elephant."

"If only." Sean let out a sigh. "An elephant would have been a snap, compared to what she asked me for."

"A snap? Just a snap?"

Oh, yes. There was definitely a smile in her voice. He liked it.

"No question about it."

"I give up. What does she want for her birthday?"

Sean took a deep breath. "She wants me to get married."

"She wants you to…" She shifted toward him. "To get married?"

"I told you, an elephant would have been a snap."

Savannah stared at him. No. It couldn't be. But everything was starting to make sense. Telling her he was going to call her his fiancée in the clothing shop. All those expensive clothes. All the talk about her playing a role.

"Wait just a minute, O'Connell. Are you saying you want me to pretend that I'm—that you and I are—"

"Engaged. You got it."

She couldn't seem to take her eyes from the crazy man sitting next to her. He wanted to pass her off as his fiancée?

"Engaged?" she repeated, in a voice that seemed to climb the scale from alto to lyric soprano.

"Uh-huh. A perfect young couple, head over heels in love."

His tone mocked the words. Why did that make her feel sad?

"Come on, McRae, don't look at me as if I asked you to stand on your head while playing the piano. This isn't rocket science. People get engaged all the time. All you have to do is—"

"No."

"You've already proved what a great actress you are. The way you came on to me that night…" His voice roughened. "All an act, right?"

"Right," she said without hesitating.

"So, what's the problem? You don't have to sleep with me, if that's what's worrying you. All I require is—"

"I said, no." Savannah sat straight in her seat and stared out the windshield. Sean had just turned onto the road that led to his hotel; the entrance was not far ahead. "As in, En Oh. There's not a way in the world I'm going to do this."

"I don't want to upset you, sugar," he said in a voice that made a lie of the promise, "but you don't have a say in the matter."

She looked at him. His profile, seen in the lights of the hotel as they approached it, was stony. And, of course, he was right. She didn't have a say, not unless she could come up with half a million dollars to repay Alain…and another half million to secure Missy's future.

How could he expect such a thing of her? To pretend to be his fiancée? Pretend she loved him, wanted him, wanted to be in his arms as she had been just a little while ago?

Pain pierced her like a forsaken dream. She swung away from him as they pulled up in front of the hotel. The parking attendant and the doorman were both hurrying toward them, just as they had last time. Everything was the same, except what Sean wanted.

"People don't do things like this," she said in a low voice.

"Thanks for that bit of insight, McRae. I don't know what I'd have done without—"

The car doors swung open simultaneously. "Good evening," the attendant said. The doorman smiled at Savannah. "Ma'am," he said pleasantly, "it's nice to see you again."

Nice? She was back at the scene of the crime. What could possibly be nice about that?

She stormed past the man but she didn't get very far. Sean grabbed her arm and led her toward the steps.

"Let go," she hissed.

"So you can run? No way, sugar. You already did that once. It's old."

"I didn't run. You threw me out. Damn it, will you let go?"

"Well, I'm not throwing you out this time," he said, hustling her inside the lobby.

"Listen, you—you egocentric fraud—"

The desk clerk looked around in surprise. So did a couple who'd been talking with him. All six eyebrows reached for their hairlines.

Why not? Sean thought grimly. They probably made an interesting sight, he damned near towing Savannah toward the elevator, she trying her best to dig in her heels and halt his progress.

"Madame? Sir? May I be of service?"

It was the desk clerk, scurrying toward them, trying to smile while looking terrified.

"No," Sean snarled.

"Yes," Savannah snapped. "Find a shrink and have this man committed."

"She has an unusual sense of humor," Sean said as he

banged on the elevator call button. When the ornate glass and silver doors opened, he pulled Savannah inside the car.

"Ma'am?" the desk clerk said uneasily, and Savannah rolled her eyes.

"Oh, for God's sake," she said, "just go away!"

The doors slid shut. Sean slid his key card into the penthouse slot and the car rose. Savannah wrenched free and glared at him. "You're good at this. Kidnapping women and shoving them around."

The doors opened again. Sean caught her by the elbow, hurried her through the entry hall and into the sitting room.

"Let me be sure I've got this right," he said. "You were willing to sleep with me but when I tell you there's no sex involved, that all you have to do is pretend to be my fiancée, you go crazy."

Crazy was exactly how it sounded, but she wasn't about to admit that.

"You want me to lie."

"Oh, I see." His lips curved in a smirk. "The McRae Morality Code frowns on lies."

"Obviously, yours doesn't."

That seemed to hit the target. Sean's shoulders fell.

"You think I'm thrilled about it, you're wrong. I just don't have a choice." He went to the minibar and opened it. "Besides, what do you care? She's my mother, not yours."

"It's not right."

"You never lied to your mother?"

"I never had to. She didn't know what I did or didn't do, and…" Savannah frowned. Why tell him that? She never talked about her life, her family. It was nobody's business, certainly not O'Connell's. "Besides, you couldn't pull it off."

Sean tossed two cans of Diet Coke, a bag of chips and a couple of candy bars on a low table.

"Eat something," he commanded.

"I'm not hungry."

"Of course you're hungry. So am I, and ordering up dried-out chicken sandwiches and coffee from the bottom of the pot doesn't appeal to me."

He opened the bag of chips and held it out. The wonderful aroma of salt and fat rose to her nostrils. To her horror, her stomach did a low, long rumble.

"Not hungry, huh?" He pushed the bag at her. "Eat."

Reluctantly, she reached in and took a handful of chips. They tasted as good as they smelled, and she took another handful.

"Why can't you just tell her you shouldn't have promised such a thing in the first place?"

He sighed, sat down on the sofa and laced his hands behind his head. The movement brought his biceps into sharp delineation. It did the same for the long muscles in his thighs and when he stretched out his legs, his black T-shirt rode up an inch, revealing a hard, flat belly.

"Because I've disappointed her too many times already."

Savannah blinked. "What?"

"You asked me why I didn't just tell her that—"

"I got that." She hesitated. "But you'd disappoint her with this anyway. Eventually, you'd have to tell her the truth."

That got him to his feet. He ran his hands through his hair until it stood up in little spikes and paced from the living room to the bedroom. Savannah followed.

"Engagements fall apart all the time. She'll accept that."

"I thought you said you'd promised her you'd get married."

"Right. I did. But…" He paused, then let out a long sigh.

"You're right, I did. Okay. I'll introduce you as my wife. I'll say—I'll say we met, went crazy for each other, eloped... Now what?"

"I told you, I don't want to do it."

His smile was quick and unpleasant. "Remember what I said about not having a choice? Well, neither do you... unless you're not interested in earning that money."

"It's an impossible plan."

In his heart, he was starting to think so, too. The last thing he needed was to hear those words from her lips.

"It'll be a cinch. We'll buy a ring. Rings. Engagement, wedding bands—one for you, one for me."

"Only a man would think that's all there is to marriage!" Savannah threw out her hands. "Has it occurred to you that we don't know the first thing about each other?"

"I thought of that. It's why I need you for two weeks. It'll give us time to get acquainted, so to speak, before my mother's birthday, and...Savannah?"

She shook her head, turned her back to him, but not before he'd seen the tears in her eyes. He went to her quickly, stepped in front of her and clasped her shoulders.

"Savannah," he said softly, "what is it?"

What, indeed? He wanted her to play a game. It was a lot better than the games she'd expected he wanted, or Alain's obscene plans. Two weeks of acting and a half-million dollar payoff. How come her heart felt as if it might break?

"Listen to me," she said desperately. "What you want us to do is a mistake."

"Then you'll do it?"

Her chin came up. "You said it yourself. I don't have much choice, do I?"

Sean looked at her. Her eyes were smudged with exhaustion; the night breeze had turned her hair into a tangle of curls and her sweatshirt bore a smattering of potato chip crumbs.

She was, in other words, even more beautiful. How could a woman be a mess and still be beautiful? No way could he figure it out.

"Why don't you have a choice?" he said, after a minute.

"That's a dumb question."

"It's the first intelligent question I've asked you." His hands cupped her shoulders. "I'm not talking about our arrangement, I'm talking about your—your relationship with Beaumont." She tried to pull away; he held her fast before him. "Why do you let him run your life? Why are you with him?"

She stared at him. Could she tell him? About herself, and her childhood. About Missy. About everything?

God, was she losing her mind? This man had all but bought her. He'd *bought* her. What could she possibly tell him that would mean a damn?

"I can't—I can't explain."

"Maybe I can help. If he has something on you—"

"Has something?"

"Yeah. You know. If you've ever done something you don't want anyone to know about. Been arrested. Been charged with—"

"You think I'm a criminal?"

"No. I don't think that. I just think there must be a reason you're with a man like that."

"I'm with him," she said flatly. "That's all."

"You despise him. And he treats you as if—as if—"

"O'Connell, I'm tired. We made a deal and I'm prepared to go through with it. You want a fiancée? You'll have one."

Her voice had turned hard. So had her eyes. Who was the

real Savannah? Was she someone who didn't think it was nice to lie, or someone who'd do anything for money?

"I want a fiancée for two weeks," he said. "Then a wife for a one-time, show-stopping performance."

"A one-night wife," she said, with a bitter smile.

"Yes. Can you manage that?"

"I can manage anything for five hundred thousand dollars," Savannah pulled away from him. "Where do I sleep?"

He looked at her for a long minute. Then he smiled, though the smile never reached his eyes.

"What if I said you sleep in my bed?"

She felt her pulse quicken, but she kept her eyes locked to his. "I thought you said—"

"Maybe I changed my mind."

Again, the seconds ticked by. She couldn't read his face at all. Did he mean it? Would he demand she sleep with him? She wouldn't do it, not for all the money in the world. She wouldn't let him undress her, caress her, take her on that journey she'd never experienced. It would be terrible. It would be...

It would be ecstasy. She'd dreamed of his hands on her breasts. His mouth on her thighs. His body, pressing her down into the softness of the bed.

Savannah raised her chin. "Maybe you want too much for the money, O'Connell."

He laughed softly. "Maybe," he said, and before she could do anything to stop him, he pulled her into his arms and kissed her. It was a kiss given without mercy, hard and demanding and, heaven help her, it was everything she wanted.

She stopped thinking, stopped wondering, stopped doing anything but feeling. She wound her arms around Sean's neck and met his explosive passion, matched it, opened her mouth to the sharp nip of his teeth. He groaned, lifted her into his erection, slid his hand under her sweatshirt, under her T-shirt and cupped her breast.

"Yes," she sobbed as he bent his head and took her nipple into his mouth. A flame seemed to shoot from her breasts straight down into her belly. She dug her hands into his hair, needing his kisses against her breast, needing them on her mouth, needing him as she had never permitted herself to need anyone.

"Sean," she whispered. "Sean, please…"

"What?" His voice was thick. "Please, what? Tell me."

"I want—I want—"

All at once, he stopped. He raised his head and looked at her through cold eyes.

"I know exactly what you want," he said. "That's good, sugar. It's very good. Thanks for letting me see you'll be as terrific in this role as you were the night we met."

"No. Sean—"

"Relax." He spoke calmly, as if they hadn't just been in each other's arms. "You won't have to take your act on the road. Hell, if you can be this convincing after a couple of kisses, why would I want you to do anything more?"

Savannah's heart seemed to stop beating. She wanted to die. She wanted *him* to die. What he'd done…

"You can have the bedroom." He looked her up and down, a satisfied little smile tugging at the corners of his mouth. "Hell, McRae, nothing's too good for a performer like you."

The smile, the cutting words, brought her back to life.

"You," she sputtered, "you—you—you—"

She grabbed a vase, flung it, watched it shatter into a million pieces as it hit the door that swung shut behind him.

"I hate you," she screamed. "I hate you, Sean O'Connell!"

Savannah buried her face in her hands and sank to the floor. What a lie! She hated him, yes, but the person she hated most was herself.

CHAPTER TEN

SEAN WAS UP well before six o'clock the next morning.

He tried phoning down for coffee. Room service, it seemed, wouldn't be able to accommodate him for another half hour.

"We do have coffee at the reception desk for our early-rising guests," the clerk told him.

Grumbling, Sean headed to the lobby, poured himself a cup of the stuff from a silver pot and glugged it down.

On the way back to the elevator, he made a pit stop in the men's room. Bad idea. The face that greeted him in the mirror wasn't pretty. He needed a shave, a shower and a way to stop scowling, but everything connected to those necessities was behind his closed bedroom door.

He went back to the desk, took the silver pot and a cup, offered a terse "You don't mind, do you?" to a clerk who looked as if he'd sooner argue with one of the crocs that inhabited the island's swampy north shore, and headed back to his suite.

Half an hour later, he was going crazy. He paced, he drank coffee, he paced some more. The coffee was his second bad idea of the morning. He could damn near feel the caffeine hightailing it through his system.

As if his nerves weren't jangling enough already.

He'd had a miserable night. The living-room sofa was too short, too soft, too everything but comfortable. He'd slept in his jeans and T-shirt, and he normally slept in his skin. Not that he'd actually slept.

How could he, considering the mess he'd created? Man, he wanted out! First the stupid pledge to Mary Elizabeth, then the even stupider determination to make good on it, and now this—this thing with Savannah...

"Hell," he muttered, running his hands through his hair.

Why had he ever imagined that he could take a stranger and pass her off as his wife? That he could make a woman like Savannah seem sweet, soft and innocent?

Except, there were moments she really did seem sweet, soft and innocent. Moments like the ones last night, when he'd taken her into his arms to prove a point, when she'd trembled at his touch before losing herself in his kisses.

Sean's jaw tightened.

An act. All of it. How come he kept forgetting that her talent for make-believe was the reason he'd thought of using her in the first place? The lady was good. Really good. Anybody seeing what had happened would have thought she meant it, that she'd really wanted him.

That he'd really wanted her.

Okay. He had. Damned right, he had. Kissing her, caressing her, had nothing to do with proving things. He kept telling himself that because it made him feel like less of a sleaze.

What kind of man lusted after a woman who made her living doing God knew what for a creep like Alain Beaumont?

Sean downed the last of the coffee. It was bitter and cold, but maybe the last jolt of caffeine would kick-start his brain. He needed to begin thinking straight. Make sense of things, starting with who and what Savannah McRae really was.

That conversation he'd walked in on when he'd boarded Beaumont's yacht. The key might be there. Beaumont had been talking about some sort of deal. She'd turned it down. No. "Turned it down" was the wrong way to phrase it. She'd been frantic. Hysterical.

Terrified.

In his anger, he'd thought she and Beaumont were just arguing over money. Truth was, they'd been fighting over more than that. Beaumont wanted her to do something. She didn't want to do it. Why hadn't she just walked out on the man? Told him what he could do with his plans, whatever they were, his yacht, his wealth?

Why was she willing to stay with such a pig?

A simple question, with a simple answer. She stayed for the life and the money. What else could it be?

Sean reached for the coffee, shuddered and pushed it aside. He'd lived among the rich and famous a good part of his life, first growing up in Vegas, then as a gambler. Some were okay people. Some weren't.

And some—only a few and almost always male—were downright monsters, certain that their wealth entitled them to live by codes of their own devising. They surrounded themselves with people who accepted that conviction. He'd seen servants who might as well have been slaves, business associates who turned a blind eye to stuff that was immoral if not downright illegal, wives willing to pretend they didn't see infidelities that were right under their noses.

He'd seen the mistresses of such men tolerate treatment that made his stomach turn.

Did that explain Savannah? He'd been sure it did, except the more he saw of her, the more he had this funny feeling that he was only seeing the surface.

And how come she was in his head all the time? How come—*be honest now, O'Connell*—he'd sought her out for this bit of subterfuge?

Forget the stuff about her acting talent. She was good,

yeah, but how tough would this performance be? One night, pretending she was his wife? With a little effort, he could come up with half a dozen women who could have carried it off and who'd have found it a lark. No metaphorical arm-twisting needed.

The truth was, he wanted her playing the part, not some other woman. There was something about her that got to him and not just sexually, although yeah, she got to him that way, too.

It was why he hadn't slept last night. The intensity of the kiss had stunned him. Those things he'd said about kissing her just to see if they'd be able to make the relationship look real was bull. The truth was, he'd let go of her because the need he'd felt to take her shocked him.

He'd never felt such hunger before.

Not that he'd solved the problem by saying something he regretted and walking away. Hell, those moments he'd had her in his arms had played in his head all night, like a loop of tape. He'd tossed and turned for hours, sweaty as a schoolboy, imagining what would have happened if he hadn't come to his senses. He thought about how it would have been to undress her. Bare her to his hands and mouth. See if all of her tasted as sweet as her high, perfect breasts.

Finally, he'd leaped from the damned sofa and stalked out to the terrace. He had a bad case of ZTS, was all. Zipper Think Syndrome, the name he and his brothers had jokingly given to the way men were led around by their anatomy.

It hadn't helped.

What he needed was either a shrink or a cold shower, but both were out of the question. You didn't go to a shrink just because you wanted a woman you shouldn't want. To get to the shower, he'd have to go through his bedroom, assuming she hadn't turned the lock. Not that it mattered. He wouldn't do it.

Even the thought of it—his bedroom, his bed, Savannah lying in it asleep, warm and sweet-smelling—was a mistake.

Or maybe the mistake had been not taking what he'd wanted, what they'd both wanted, last night...

"If you want to get into your bedroom, it's all yours."

Savannah stood in the bedroom doorway wearing her jeans and sweatshirt. Idly, he wondered if she'd slept in her clothes, same as him.

From the look on her face, Sean knew they were still at war. Maybe it was time to declare a truce. How else were they going to get through the next two weeks?

"Thanks," he said, trying for a neutral tone.

"There's nothing to thank me for." She strode past him. "I'll see you around."

She'd see him around? Anger shot through him and he moved past her and blocked the door.

"What the hell does that mean?"

"It means I'm leaving. It's what I should have done last night."

"You can't leave. We have an arrangement."

"Not anymore. I thought things through, O'Connell. I can't do this."

"Maybe you didn't understand me. I said, we have a deal."

Savannah's eyes flashed. "Get out of my way."

"You owe me money. Is this how you repay your debts?"

"I don't owe you anything."

"Sure you do. Two weeks ago you laid it on the line... and lost."

Her face colored. "I tried to keep my end of that wager, O'Connell. You sent me away."

She was right, but what did being right have to do with anything? They had a deal.

"How about Beaumont?"

"What about him?" she said, but the color began draining from her cheeks.

"Give me a break, okay? I don't know exactly what I walked in on the other night, but I suspect he's not gonna be happy to see you."

Not happy to see her? The depth of Sean's understatement almost made her laugh. She still wasn't sure how she'd handle Alain; all she could hope was that he'd calmed down. Surely, he didn't really want to use her as a—a prize in a tournament.

He'd be past such craziness by now. He'd agree to let her play cards to win back the money, to let Missy stay in Switzerland, to remember that once he'd treated her with courtesy and kindness.

Right. And polar ice caps floated in the Caribbean.

"Well?" Sean folded his arms. "I don't hear you telling me Beaumont will greet you with open arms."

"That's not your problem." She jerked her chin at the door. "Please step aside."

Sean hesitated. *Stop her,* a voice inside him said. *What for?* another voice replied. So what if she left? The entire plan was a bad idea.

He shrugged and did as she'd asked. "Go on. Just be sure and tell your boyfriend he still owes me."

Savannah swung toward him, her face livid. "He's not my boyfriend."

"Whatever you say, sugar."

"He's not!"

"Yeah, whatever. Just tell him I expect my money within 24 hours, now that you've reneged on the deal he and I made."

"Damn you," she said, her voice so low he had to strain to hear it. "Damn you to hell, Sean O'Connell! Do you hear yourself? Do you hear what you're saying?'' Sean jerked back in surprise as she jabbed her finger into the center of his chest. "The deal you and he made. The deal *you* and *Alain* made!" Another jab, followed by a flat hand slamming against him. "How dare you, you—you no-good son of a bitch? How dare you think you can treat me like—like a streetwalker?''

"Hey. Wait just a minute. I didn't—"

"Yeah, you did." She slammed him with her fist this time, and she wasn't gentle about it. "Buying me!"

"Whoa," Sean said, holding up a hand. "I did not buy you."

"You want to get technical about it? No. You didn't. You—you made a deal with Alain."

"No way," he said, with all the self-righteous indignation of a man who knows he's wrong. "Your boyfriend—"

Without warning, her fist slammed into his belly with enough force to make the air whoosh from his lungs.

"He—is—not—my—boyfriend! He's a monster. How can you even suggest such a thing? I loathe him. Loathe him, loathe...."

Tears poured down her cheeks. Sean cursed and pulled her into his arms. She was crying as if the world were about to end and it damn neared killed him. He'd been fooling himself, trying to pretend all he wanted was to make love to her when the truth was, he wanted to protect her from whatever demons stalked her.

Gently, he lifted her face to his and kissed her. She shook her head wildly but he ignored it and kissed her again, holding her as if she were precious because she was, and he was done with trying to figure out why he should feel that way about her.

He kept kissing her, stroking his hand down her spine.

When she sighed and leaned into him, he felt as if he'd beat back those demons, at least for the moment.

The kiss deepened. Her mouth clung to his. Her hands slipped up his chest; her fingers curled in the soft cotton of his shirt and Sean knew there was no sense in kidding himself.

He'd started this to comfort Savannah but comfort was the last thought in his head right now. She tasted like honey, smelled as sweet as summer, and they fit one against the other like matching pieces of a jigsaw puzzle just begun.

His need for her was almost overpowering.

But he couldn't, wouldn't let her know that. She wasn't herself. She was in pain. In despair. She was weeping. He'd done so many wrong things since they'd met, he wasn't going to add taking advantage of her to the list.

"Sweetheart." His voice was so rough he was amazed he could talk at all. Carefully, he held her by the shoulders and took a single step back. "Savannah. Let me just...let me just—"

"Sean," she whispered and rose to him, clasping his face, bringing his mouth to hers, and he was lost.

A torrent of desire flooded his senses. He groaned and swung her into his arms, never taking his mouth from hers as he carried her into the bedroom and laid her down on the bed that was still warm from her body.

When he drew back, she gave a little cry of distress and he took her hands and pressed kisses into the palms.

"Are you sure?" he whispered.

"I've never been surer of anything in my life." Tears still glittered on her lashes, but her lips curved in a smile. "Make love to me, Sean. Please."

He undressed her slowly, kissing each bit of skin as he bared it to his mouth. Her sighs, her moans, the beat of his heart became the only sounds in the universe.

When she was naked, he spent a long moment just looking at her, the delicacy of her breasts, the gentle rounding of her belly, the gold of her skin, but she stirred uneasily and when his gaze moved to her face, he saw a shadow in her eyes. Wariness. Trepidation.

Fear.

Was she afraid of what he might do to her? Had Beaumont...? No. He wasn't going to think about that son of a bitch. Not now. Now, all that mattered was Savannah.

"Savannah," he whispered urgently, "don't be afraid. I'll never hurt you."

She shook her head. "I'm not afraid of you. But—but there's something I should tell you—"

"No," he said, silencing her with a kiss. What she was going to say, that she'd been with a lot of other men, that some of them had done things... He didn't want to hear it. Didn't need to hear it. All he needed was this. Her mouth. Her breasts. The way he could make her breath catch when he licked her nipples. The way she moaned when he slid his hands under her, lifted her to him, kissed her belly, her thighs.

"Sean. Oh God, Sean..."

She was trembling again, but not with fear. With passion. The intensity of her need for him filled him with joy. This was how he wanted her. Open to him. Wanting him.

Him. Only him.

He kept his eyes on hers as parted her thighs. She moaned; her eyes went wide as he stroked a finger over her labia. She cried out, jolted like a filly who'd never before carried a rider.

"Sweet," he whispered. "So sweet..."

Slowly, carefully, he opened her to him. Breathed lightly against the waiting bud that had bloomed for him. Kissed it. Caressed it, and suddenly she arched like a bow. Her cry soared into the heavens and she sobbed his name.

Sean pulled off his clothes and came down to her. Caught her hands, entwined his fingers with hers, watched her face, her beautiful face, as he moved between her thighs and entered her...

And discovered that his lover was a virgin.

The realization shocked him into immobility. "Savannah?"

A world of questions were in that one word. Savannah understood them all and knew she'd have to provide answers but for now, only one mattered.

"Sean." She sighed his name, lifted her head and bit lightly into his shoulder. The taste of man and musk quickened the race of her already-galloping heart. "Please. Make love to me."

Groaning with pleasure, Sean slid into her warmth and took her with him to the stars.

THEY LAY TANGLED TOGETHER, breathing raggedly, a fine film of sweat drying on their skin.

"You're a virgin," he said in wonderment.

"Not anymore," she said softly, her lips curving at the awe in his voice, at the joy in her heart, and felt his lips curve, too, against her throat.

"You should have told me."

"Oh, sure. There's always an easy way to bring something like that into the conversation."

"I'd have gone slower."

"Mmm. Slower sounds nice."

Her words were a teasing purr. Sean smiled again and bit lightly into her flesh.

"Are you all right?"

"Yes." She moved beneath him, stretching like a cat. "I'm very all right."

He lifted his head. Her face was inches from his. Her eyes glowed and her smile would definitely have tempted Da Vinci. She looked sated and happy, and his heart did a little two-step of absolute male satisfaction.

"I'm glad. Still, if I'd known…"

"Would you have believed me?"

A muscle knotted in his jaw. After a couple of seconds, he turned on his side but kept his arm tightly around her.

"No."

Savannah nodded. His honesty was one of the things she liked about Sean O'Connell. It was a rare quality.

"I'm sorry, Savannah. I know you wanted me to say I would have, but—"

She rolled toward him and put her finger across his mouth. "Don't apologize for speaking the truth. Of course you wouldn't have believed me." She traced the outline of his lips. "Why on earth would you?"

Sean sucked her finger between his teeth and bit down gently. Then he took her hand from his mouth and kissed it.

"So, he isn't—"

"No." Savannah shuddered. "God, no. He's not."

"Then, what is he to you? Your business partner?"

"Alain is…Alain was—" she said, hastily correcting the error "—he was my friend."

"Beaumont?"

She could hear the incredulity in his voice. She couldn't blame him. The man Alain had recently revealed himself to be couldn't be anyone's friend, but the Alain she knew— the one she thought she knew—was different.

"I met him a long time ago," she said, propping herself

on her elbows so she could see Sean's face. ''He was—he was good to me.''

''Oh, yeah. He sounded like he was being good to you the other night, all right. Almost as good as the night he sent you to seduce me.''

''He didn't tell me to—to go to bed with you that night,'' Savannah said quickly.

''No,'' Sean said coldly. ''He just told you to keep me so busy thinking about taking you to bed that I wouldn't concentrate on the game.''

''He's changed. The Alain I knew... That Alain isn't there anymore.''

The Alain she'd *thought* she knew, Sean told himself, and what did she mean, he'd been good to her? From the little he'd seen, Beaumont treated her like dirt.

''How was he good to you?''

''What?''

''You said he was good to you. I'm trying to figure out how.''

There was an edge to his voice. He wanted explanations but how could she give them? She wasn't ready to talk to him about Missy or the way she and her sister had lived. Lying naked in the arms of a man she hardly knew seemed less intimate than telling him the ugly details of her life.

''He just was,'' she said stiffly, and started to pull away. Sean drew her close again.

''I'm sorry.''

''Let me up, please.''

''No.'' Gently, he pushed her onto her back. ''I'm a fool,'' he said gruffly, ''talking about Beaumont when we have so many other things to discuss.''

He kissed her. She tried not to respond but he kissed her again and she felt her resolve slipping.

"What things?" she said softly, brushing his hair back from his forehead.

"Important things." His voice grew husky. "The way you taste." He kissed her again, gently parting her lips with his. "I love the way you taste."

She smiled. "Do you?"

"Uh-huh. Your mouth." He dipped his head, touched the tip of his tongue to the hollow in her throat. "Your throat." He dipped his head again and licked one nipple, then the other. "And your breasts. You have beautiful breasts, Savannah."

Her breath caught as his teeth closed lightly on one pink bud. "When you do that…when you do that…"

"I love the feel of your nipples on my tongue."

"Oh God. Sean…"

"What?"

He looked up. Her eyes were becoming dark; the color in her face was rising. Her skin was turning warm and fragrant and his heart was doing flip-flops in his chest. He brought his mouth to hers, whispered his desire.

"Savannah. I want to make love to you again."

She cupped his face, kissed him, openmouthed, sighed his name against his lips.

"Is it too soon? I don't want to hurt you."

"You won't. Not by making love to me. I want you to. I want—"

She cried out as he slipped his hand between her thighs.

"This?" he said thickly. "Is this what you want?"

"Yes. That. Oh, and that. And—and—"

He entered her on one long, deep thrust. She sobbed his name and wrapped her legs around his waist. He moved and the world shattered, shattered again as she took him deeper inside her. And when he threw back his head, cried out and exploded inside her, Savannah wept, not with sorrow but with joy.

Why had she thought this man was a stranger? How could he be, when she had waited a lifetime to find him?

CHAPTER ELEVEN

SAVANNAH CAME AWAKE slowly, her muscles filled with a delicious lassitude. Eyes still closed, she reached for Sean…

And found the space beside her empty. Sean was gone, and from the feel of the linens, he'd been gone for quite a while.

She sat up against the headboard, clutching the duvet to her breasts. In the air-conditioned silence of the room, she felt the sudden chill of being alone…and the foolishness of what she'd done last night.

What time was it? Ten o'clock, at least. The sun slanting in through the blinds had the feel of midmorning. Was that the reason she felt so disoriented? Or was it because she'd spent the night in bed with a man she barely knew?

Savannah closed her eyes. What on earth had she been thinking?

Quickly, she swung her feet to the floor.

Sleeping with Sean had only made things more confused. He already had a low opinion of her. What had happened surely wouldn't have made it better. Plus, he'd hired her to do a job. There was nothing personal in the make-believe story they were going to create.

By now, he was sure to have as many regrets as she did. Or—or maybe she was wrong. Maybe making love hadn't been a mistake.

"You're awake."

One look at Sean and she knew she'd had it right the first time.

He stood in the doorway, beautiful enough to make her skin prickle and removed enough to make his thoughts apparent. Arms folded, feet crossed at the ankles, his smile polite and remote, she knew immediately that he regretted what had happened.

So be it.

"Yes." She forced an answering smile as she drew the covers nearer her chin. "Sorry to have slept so late."

He shrugged. "No problem."

"You probably have a million things to do and here I am, keeping you from them."

Another shrug. "We have all day."

"Right." She hesitated. How long could you hold a smile until the muscles in your face froze? "Well, if you give me a few minutes—"

"Sure."

But he didn't move. Did he expect her to get up in front of him? Head for the bathroom, naked? It wasn't going to happen.

Enough. Savannah narrowed her eyes.

"I'd appreciate some privacy."

"Oh." He stood away from the door jamb and nodded. "I'll be in the sitting room."

"Fine. Ten minutes, I'll be out of your way."

"You're not in—"

"Oh, give me a break," she snapped, her patience gone. "Yes, I'm in your way. Yes, we're wasting time. The sooner you leave, the sooner I can get moving."

Something flickered across his face. Discomfort? Embarrassment? Whatever it was, she didn't give a damn. All she wanted was to see his back as he closed the door behind him.

"Uh, the stuff we bought… It got here a while ago."

"What? Oh. The clothes." Somehow, the thought of that stack of boxes, all of them holding things he'd purchased to turn her into someone she wasn't, made her feel angrier. "Fine. You pick out something you'd like me to wear and leave it on the chair, okay?"

"The clothes are yours, Savannah. You make the choice."

"They're not mine."

"Damn it, what is this? I come in to say good morning and next thing I know, I'm involved in an argument." His jaw shot forward. "They're yours," he said coldly. "Is that clear?"

"A lot of things are clear," she said, just as coldly. "Funny how daylight can make that happen."

"What the hell are you talking about?"

"Oh, for God's sake! Will you just get out of here?"

His mouth thinned. "Yeah. I'll do that."

The door closed with a bang. She grabbed a pillow and flung it across the room. She hadn't expected roses and champagne this morning but O'Connell could have been a little nicer. Couldn't he have pretended that last night—that last night—

Savannah shot to her feet. "To hell with you, Sean O'Connell," she muttered, hating herself for sounding as if she were going to burst into tears.

The duvet tangled around her legs as she stomped toward the bathroom and she tugged at it without mercy, which only made things worse. Words she'd learned years ago on the New Orleans streets hissed from her lips just as the door flew open.

"Damn you, Savannah McRae," Sean said, and pulled her roughly into his arms.

"Let me go. O'Connell, I swear, if you don't let me go—"

"Shut up," he commanded, tunneling his hands into her hair, holding her face to his so he could kiss her. His mouth was hot, his kisses deep and dangerous and with a little cry, she gave up fighting and kissed him back.

"I'm sorry," he whispered, his lips a breath from hers.

"So am I. I thought you regretted last night."

Sean kissed her again. "I did," he said bluntly, framing her face with his hands. "I told myself making love was a mistake. That we should have stuck to business." His eyes dropped to her parted lips, then met hers again. "It took a while before I was ready to admit the only mistake I've made since the minute I saw you was trying to pretend I didn't want you."

Savannah gave a watery smile. "Me, too," she said, and rose on her toes to press her mouth to his.

Long moments later, Sean clasped her hands, kissed them and brought them to his chest.

"I took your virginity."

"No," she said, shaking her head. "I gave it to you."

His smile was soft and sweet. "I almost went crazy sitting out there, telling myself what a bastard I was." His voice roughened. "Truth is, I'm glad you did. It means everything to me, sugar, knowing you gave me such a gift."

"Sometimes—sometimes I used to think it was the only part of me that was still worth anything, you know? That I'd done so many things over the years—"

He silenced her with another tender kiss. "I haven't been an angel, either. Besides, the one thing I'm certain of is that whatever you've done, you did because you had to."

Sighing, she let him draw her close against him, closed her eyes under the restful stroke of his hand down her spine.

"You're a good man, Sean O'Connell."

A deep laugh rumbled through his chest. "I've been called a lot of things, sweetheart, but that's a first." Gently, he pressed a kiss into her hair. "You know what else I thought about while you were sleeping?" She leaned back in his embrace and shook her head. "I thought how I could stop wasting time regretting something so wonderful, wake you with my kisses and make love to you again."

"Mmm. Sounds lovely."

"But—"

"But?"

Sean tipped her face up to his. "But," he said, smiling into her eyes, "if we don't eat some real food soon, all my get-up-and-go will have gotten-up-and-gone."

She laughed. It was, he thought, one of the loveliest sounds he'd ever heard. He touched the tip of his finger to her mouth.

"Plus, we have an appointment at noon."

"We do?"

"Uh-huh. And that means you have little more than an hour to get ready."

"I'll be quick."

His smile turned devastatingly sexy. "We can save time by showering together."

"I don't think that would work."

"No. Probably not." He stepped back. "Okay. I'll get those boxes. You take your shower."

Savannah kissed him, then started for the bathroom, but she turned back when Sean spoke.

"The thing is," he said gruffly. "The thing is, Savannah, I've been a loner all my life. It's tough, letting somebody in."

She knew it wasn't a line that would rank high in the annals of romantic declarations but it made the last of her reserve slip away. She knew what it took for him to say

such a thing because it was true of her, too. It was the reason
she'd panicked when she woke and he wasn't there, why
she'd done everything she could to make herself believe the
night had been an error.

Somehow, she kept her tears from flowing. "Yes," she
whispered. "I know."

Sean's face took on a taut, hungry look. "To hell with
getting things done quickly," he said, and scooped her into
his arms. And, as he carried her to the bed, Savannah knew
that what they'd just admitted to each other had the power
to heal them both...

Or to destroy them.

THEY HAD BREAKFAST on the terrace. Afterward, Sean made
a phone call. He was changing the time of their appointment, he said, but he wouldn't tell her more until they were
in his car, speeding down a narrow dirt road toward the sea.

"We're meeting with a Realtor," he said casually.

Savannah stared at him. "You're buying a house?"

"Sure," he said, as if people decided to buy homes on
islands in the Bahamas all the time. He flashed her a quick
smile and added that he'd been thinking, on and off, about
buying a place here for a while.

"Ah. So you set up this appointment a while back."

"Weeks ago."

It was a lie, though he didn't know why he was lying.
He'd made the appointment this morning, even while he
paced the living room and tried to figure out what in hell
he was getting himself into.

But, he'd told himself, it made sense, didn't it, to own
property here? He'd been investing in expensive real estate
for a long time. Nobody in his family knew it—why spoil
their conviction that he was as impractical as he was foot-
loose?—but the fact was, he could give up gambling at the

drop of a hat and still live as comfortably as any of the rest
of the O'Connells.

There just wasn't any reason to give up gambling. He
loved the risk, the emotional highs, had never found anything to give him that same thrill.

Until now.

That thought, unbidden, unwanted and terrifying, had almost sent him into the bedroom to wake Savannah, pay her
the half-mil and tell her sorry, sweets, the deal is off.

But it was too late for that. He'd come this far; he'd see
his scheme through. And yes, buying a place made sense
considering one of the reasons he'd given himself two
weeks with Savannah before his mother's birthday party was
so they could get to know each other well enough to be
convincing as lovers.

Sorry. As husband and wife.

How could they manage that in the sterile environment
of a hotel? You weren't really yourself in a hotel, no matter
how elegant. Maybe because it *was* so elegant. They'd get
acquainted better if they were alone.

So he'd phoned the Realtor, told her exactly the kind of
property he wanted and set up the appointment.

He'd felt good after that call. He'd buy a place on the
beach. Hire someone to come in and pick up the place,
maybe cook, but that was it. There'd be nothing to intrude
on the private little world he and Savannah were about to
create.

Whoa, he'd thought. What was that all about? He didn't
need a private world with anybody, he only needed the right
setting to make this stunt work.

He'd reached for the phone to cancel the appointment. He
could buy a house anytime, and really, how much of a
bother would it be to have maids or clerks or other guests

around? He and Savannah could still set the groundwork for their make-believe marriage.

That was when he'd heard her stirring. He'd gone into the bedroom to be sure she understood that what had happened the previous night wouldn't happen again.

Instead, his heart had turned over at the sight of her, looking early-morning beautiful and vulnerable as she did her best, like him, to pretend the night hadn't meant a thing.

For the first time in his life, Sean had known he was tired of taking risks that put nothing but money on the line. He'd wanted to take Savannah in his arms, and he had. He'd even told her part of what he was feeling, how he'd always been a loner, but there was more. He knew that. He just didn't know, exactly, what else he wanted to say...

"Is that the house?"

Sean dragged his attention back to the road. A handsome wrought-iron fence rose ahead, a discreet For Sale sign on a stake beside it. A small TV camera, high in a tree just beyond the gate, angled toward them as he slowed the car. The gates swung open, revealing a crushed oyster-shell drive shaded by thickets of sea grape, bougainvillea and prickly-pear cactus.

The Realtor was waiting for them on the wide marble steps of an enormous, elegant house.

Sean bent his head toward Savannah's as he helped her from the car. "Do you like it?" he said softly.

She hesitated, then smiled. "It's beautiful."

Yes, he thought, it was, but it reminded him of a hotel. A hotel for two, perhaps, but a hotel just the same. He put his arm around her and when they reached the steps, he shook the Realtor's hand.

"Mr. O'Connell," the woman said pleasantly. "I'm delighted to meet you."

Sean nodded. "My pleasure." His arm tightened around Savannah. "This is Miss McRae. My fiancée."

He felt Savannah's muscles jerk, felt the sudden tension radiate through his body at his use of the word. The Realtor's smile broadened.

"How nice! And where are you folks staying right now?"

"At the *Petite Fleur*," Sean said pleasantly, "but we're hoping to move as soon as we find a house to buy." Savannah damn near jumped. He drew her closer. "Right, Savannah?"

She looked stunned but she managed a quick "yes." It troubled him that she didn't really seem all that thrilled. Should he have told her his plans ahead of time instead of keeping them as a surprise? Why had he wanted to surprise her, anyway?

Could it have been because he was still surprising himself?

"The people who built this house were very well-known on the international scene." The Realtor leaned closer. "I'm sure you'll recognize the name. They were very happy here. They did lots of entertaining. Well, you can see it's a perfect place for that. The former owners had a staff of six—"

"Six?"

"But you'd need extra help for big parties, of course."

So much for privacy but then, if Savannah liked it...

"Yeah," Sean said, "of course."

"Let me show you through the house. I'm sure you'll both love it."

Savannah didn't. Sean could tell, even though she said all the right things. He was coming to know his pretend-fiancée's expressions. Right now, she wore a smile like a mask.

What didn't she like? He had no opinion, one way or the other. Okay, maybe he did. Truth was, growing up in overblown Las Vegas, he might have preferred something smaller. Simpler. A place where he could be himself, and she could be...

His gut tightened. Savannah would only spend the next couple of weeks here. She didn't have to love the place. It just made him wonder, was all, why she didn't.

Was it because she was accustomed to the *Lorelei?* Did she want gold cupids, dark wainscoting and crimson velvet? No. He'd watched her reaction to the things the clerk showed her at the shop in *Bijou*. The simpler, the more classic, the better.

What was it, then? Was it the prospect of the two of them rattling around alone here? The house was isolated on acres of property with nothing but shore and seabirds for company. There'd be servants—that cast of six—but well-trained servants would know how to be unobtrusive.

The more he thought about it, the more likely that seemed. Why kid himself? Alone, what would they do? What would they talk about? It wasn't as if he couldn't clue her in on things that would make them seem a real couple in the comfort of the hotel.

As good as last night had been, it was only sex. Being in bed would only get them so far. There were two weeks ahead of mornings, afternoons and evenings. Two weeks of empty hours to fill.

Why had he figured they'd be better off living alone than in the hotel?

Sean interrupted the Realtor midway through a spiel about the joys of the restaurant-size kitchen range.

"Thanks," he said. "I'll be in touch."

The look on her face mirrored Savannah's. He was lying and all of them knew it.

"Of course," the woman said, sounding disappointed.

Hey, he thought coolly, she would be, losing a six-figure commission.

Savannah looked relieved.

It made him angry as hell. She should have told him she didn't want to be alone with him right away, he thought grimly as he hustled her to the car.

"If you didn't want to move out of the hotel," he growled, "you should have said so."

She shot him a surprised look. "How could I? You said you were buying a house. You never mentioned you expected us to live in it."

"Well, you can stop worrying. We won't."

"Good." Savannah folded her arms and glared straight ahead. Why was *he* so ticked off? She was the one who had the right to be angry. He'd decided to buy a house. Well, that was his affair. That he'd decided to move her into it was hers. Why hadn't he told her? To spring something like that, to let the Realtor think they were a pair of starstruck lovers... "Living together here wasn't part of our deal."

"You're right. It wasn't." The tires squealed as Sean turned onto the main road at a speed that made trees blur as they sped past them. "I had an idea we'd find it easier to get to know each other away from the hotel. It was dumb."

"You should have asked me."

"I said, it was a dumb plan."

Seconds passed. Savannah shifted in her seat. "I can see where you'd think it made sense."

He looked at her. She was sitting as stiff as a ramrod, her profile as stern as that of the sixth-grade teacher who'd sent him to the principal's office when she'd discovered him teaching a couple of his buddies how to play craps.

"Yeah?"

"Uh-huh. I mean, if we were actually engaged, we'd want to spend time alone."

Sean nodded. "That was my thinking but, like I said, it was—"

"Did you really like that house?"

Sean looked at her again. She'd turned toward him, eyes filled with defiance.

"Why?"

"For heaven's sake, O'Connell, just answer the question. Did you like it?"

"No," he said bluntly. "It was—"

"Too big."

"Well, yes."

"Too formal."

"Right again."

"If we were a couple, if we really—if we really were lovers, would we want to live in a place so huge we'd need to leave trails of bread crumbs to find each other?"

Sean grinned. "My sentiments exactly."

She nodded and looked straight ahead again. "See? If you hadn't sprung this on me, if you'd said, 'Savannah, I think we should live someplace away from the artificial climate of a hotel so we can get to know each other better, and how would you feel living in a house the size of the Taj Mahal,' we wouldn't be having this quarrel now."

She was trying her best to sound pragmatic but what she sounded was quintessentially female. Sean's grin widened.

"Is that what we're doing? Having a quarrel?"

Something in his voice made her look at him. "Aren't we?"

"Our first."

"You're kidding. We've done nothing but quarrel since we met."

"Our first as lovers," he said, pulling under a tall palm

tree on the side of the road and shutting off the engine. He undid his seat belt, leaned over and gently undid hers. "Because that's what we are," he said softly. "We're lovers, Savannah."

"You know what I meant. I meant if we were—"

Sean gathered Savannah into his arms and kissed her. She tried not to respond but his mouth was sweet and his body was warm, and it took less than a heartbeat for her to sigh and kiss him back.

"We're lovers," he said, stroking the curls back from her cheek and tucking them behind her ear. "Even the Realtor could see that."

"It was a logical conclusion, O'Connell. You introduced me as your fiancée."

"Yeah." Sean took her hand and lifted it to his lips. "Which reminds me…we have to make the trip to Bijou again."

"No way. As it is, you bought enough clothes for ten of me!"

He chuckled. "If my sisters heard you say that, they'd hustle you off to a psychiatrist."

"Oh, right. You mentioned them before. Two sisters?"

"Three, and every last one of them would—well, maybe that's an overstatement. Two of 'em, for sure, would tell you a beautiful woman can never have too many things in her closet."

That won him a little smile. "Honestly. I don't need anything. You bought me so much—"

"A ring."

Her eyes widened. "A what?"

"A ring." Sean kissed her hand again, then gently sucked the tip of her ring finger into his mouth. "Men who are engaged to be married give their fiancées engagement rings."

"Don't be silly. They don't. Not always."

"Always," he said firmly, deliberating ignoring the fact that one of his brothers hadn't married conventionally enough to have time to put a ring on his fiancée's finger. It was a reasonable demand, wasn't it? He had a mother, an entire family, to fool.

A ring. His ring, on her finger. It would only be part of the game, but...

Savannah leaned her forehead against his. "Sean. This—this is getting complicated."

"I'm just trying to make sure we seem believable."

She looked up. "Is that the reason you made love to me last night? So we'd seem—"

His kiss left her dizzy.

"You know it wasn't," he said gruffly. "I made love to you for the same reason you made love to me, because we need to be together as much as we need to breathe."

Need, Savannah thought. He'd said need. As if what they'd shared would go on. As if they had a future that stretched further ahead than two short weeks.

She sighed, closed her eyes and buried her face against his throat.

"Complicated," she whispered, with a little catch in her voice.

This time, he didn't argue. She was right but he didn't want to talk about that now or even think about it. Instead, he held her close, reveled in the feel of her in his arms, and wondered if he'd ever, in all his life, felt so complete.

"Savannah?"

"Hmm?"

"You said I should have asked you what kind of house you preferred. Well, I'm asking."

"I didn't say that. Not exactly. What I said was—"

"There's a place up the road a couple of miles. I saw the

For Sale sign and drove in for a quick look the last time I was here. I haven't seen the inside but from the outside…'' He took a breath. Why did he feel so nervous? All he was doing was describing a house. ''It's small. Well, compared to the monster we just saw, it is. Three bedrooms, maybe four.''

Savannah's smile was as bright as the sky. ''Darn,'' she said softly. ''You mean, we wouldn't need six strangers underfoot to keep things going?''

''Just you and me,'' Sean murmured, stroking the back of his hand down her cheek. ''Truth is, the house is beautiful. And it's on the beach, comes with maybe five, six acres of land you'd need a machete to get through.''

''We'd have privacy.''

Sean nodded. ''Yes. All we could ask for. There's a pool, a small garden, a conservatory like the one Cullen has at his place on Nantucket.''

''Who?''

God, there was so much she didn't know about him, so much he didn't know about her…but there was time to learn. There was plenty of time, and he was looking forward to every second.

''One of my brothers. Cull lives in Boston with his wife and baby, but he has a house on the Atlantic and this room I've always liked. Glass walls, a big telescope. He can watch the ocean, see whales and dolphins and—''

He fell silent, suddenly feeling foolish. Maybe Savannah thought whales and dolphins were kid stuff. But she smiled, and the way she smiled set his concerns to rest.

''I love to watch whales and dolphins! Whales, especially. The way they seem to dance in the sea, you know? I never get tired of seeing them, even if Alain always says I'm foolish to—to…''

Her words trailed away. For a moment, Beaumont seemed

to be in the car with them, his presence a stain on the bright afternoon. The questions in Sean's head fought to surface, but what mattered right now was the sudden darkness in Savannah's eyes.

He gathered her close and kissed her until the darkness was gone and they were alone again in their make-believe universe.

"Beaumont's out of your life forever, sweetheart," he said. "I promise."

Because she had already learned that Sean would never lie to her, because the sun was shining down from a cloudless sky, but mostly because she was safe in her lover's arms, Savannah did a foolish thing.

She let herself believe it.

CHAPTER TWELVE

SEAN CALLED THE REALTOR on his cell phone. Yes, she said happily, she knew the property he meant and it was still on the market.

She met them at the foot of a long, winding driveway. A couple of hours later, the deal was done.

The house was his.

Though he already owned other properties, this was the first time he'd bought one to live in, the first time he'd wanted to do that…and, most definitely, the first time he'd wanted to share his space with a woman.

The realization shook him. He reminded himself that this was all simply a logical part of a plan. Still, he felt almost unbearably happy when he saw the excitement and pleasure that glowed in Savannah's eyes as they walked through the house together the next day.

"It's beautiful," she said.

Beautiful, indeed. Sean couldn't get enough of looking at her.

The house came furnished. A good thing, because they moved in right away. Standing on the porch, Sean wondered what it would be like if this weren't make-believe. If they were really moving in together.

If the diamond ring he'd bought and slipped on her finger, and the matching wedding band he intended to surprise her with once they headed for Vegas, weren't part of a plan but marked a turning point in his life.

The thought shocked him. Horrified him. What kind of craziness was this? He wanted this woman, yes, but he'd wanted other women. This relationship only seemed special because of the circumstances.

That was all it was, he told himself, and he swung Savannah into his arms and headed for the bedroom. Laughing, she clung to his shoulders.

"What are you doing, O'Connell?"

"It's an old Irish custom," he said with a lightness he didn't feel. "We have to inaugurate the bed for good luck."

Long moments later, they lay spent in each other's arms, Sean staring up at the ceiling and knowing that it was time to stop lying to himself.

What he felt for Savannah *was* special. Two truths revealed in one day. What in hell was happening to him?

Maybe it was safer not to find out.

THE HOUSE WAS PERFECT, eight big rooms with walls of glass. Anywhere you stood, you could look at the pink sand and deep blue sea, or at the rich tangle of green that shielded the estate from the world.

The shower room in the master bath had glass walls, too. Standing inside it, warm water cascading down your body, you could turn your face up to the hot yellow sun by day, the cold white stars by night.

It was as perfect a place, Sean said huskily, to love each other as the bed.

That first night, standing in the shower, her lover's moon-washed eyes looking into hers, his hands molding her to him as he caressed her breasts, then laved them with his tongue, Savannah trembled.

"What is it, sweetheart?" Sean murmured.

She shook her head. She was happy. So happy that admitting it might be dangerous.

Sean could have told her he understood. He read what she was thinking, what she was feeling, in her eyes and knew those emotions were inside his own heart.

"Savannah," he said huskily. "Savannah, I—I—"

The words he needed were there. So close. So very close. He just couldn't find them. He only knew that whatever was happening to her was happening to him, too.

It was magic, and only a fool would try putting a name to magic.

SAVANNAH HAD NEVER LIVED with a man before.

Her years with Alain didn't count. She'd been a guest on his yacht and in his chateau, always with a room and bath of her own and no greater connection to him than to the servants who attended him.

Now, she knew she hadn't been a guest at all. She'd been a servant, a different kind of servant, but that was what she'd been. His cook prepared meals, his maid cleaned, his chauffeur drove his big black limousine…

And she was a source of amusement.

All this time she'd let herself think she was valuable to him because she played cards so well. The truth, which she'd only just started admitting to herself, was that she was good but Alain was better. Aside from that, she'd been his clever pet. A puppy taken from the streets, cleaned up, taught manners and little tricks.

He'd liked teaching her which fork to use, which wine to drink because it made him feel superior. But most of all, he'd liked watching her sit at a table filled with important men and beat them at cards because the men all thought he was the reason she was so skilled.

Now, it would give him a bigger kick to sell her to them.

Horrid as the thought was, she knew it was the truth. That was what he'd intended all along. Alain had simply used what had happened with Sean as an excuse to move up the calendar.

Was he sick? Evil? She didn't care. Fate had given her the chance to escape and she was going to take it.

It was the same fate that had given her Sean O'Connell—and would, she was certain, eventually take him from her.

Winning streaks never lasted.

The longer they lived together in the house on the beach, the more terrible that truth became.

Savannah told herself not to think about it. To enjoy these days. These nights. To be happy.

Oh, and she was happy! It didn't matter what they did. Dance in one of the island's beautiful clubs, walk the beach barefoot, dine in an elegant restaurant, have conch burgers at a little shack Sean knew near the harbor, or grill lobsters when the sun sank into the sea, whatever they did was wonderful. Her lover was wonderful. And she—she—

Savannah's thoughts skittered in panic. She what? Feelings were dangerous things. Life had taught her that early on. What she felt for Sean was affection. Gratitude. Respect. There was no sense in trying to make more of it than it was.

She did love being with him. It was safe to use the word that way. He seemed to enjoy being with her, too. True to his promise, they spent their days learning about each other. He was a meat-and-potatoes guy. She preferred salads. He liked watching documentaries on TV. She liked watching old movies. He liked chess. She'd never played the game. He taught her and after a slow start, their games often ended in stalemates.

He also adored rough-and-tumble sports. She learned that the hard way, when he swore up and down one rainy night that there was nothing on their satellite TV but football, rugby and soccer.

"Liar," she said huffily, snatching the remote from him

and clicking through the channels until she found a pair of women earnestly discussing how to get in touch with your inner self. She suffered through five minutes of it until Sean groaned and held his hands over his ears. Then she giggled, flung herself on him and said there were really better ways to get in touch with your inner self.

And he obliged. They loved and played and avoided anything serious…until one morning. They were having breakfast on the patio—mangoes from a roadside stand, croissants from a bakery in *Bijou*—when Sean suddenly asked her a question. "Tell me about yourself," he said.

The question took her by surprise. She looked up from her plate and flashed a quick smile.

"There's not much left to tell. I mean, you already know I can't cook worth a hill of beans. Remember those conch fritters?"

She grinned but he wasn't going to let her off. She knew it as soon as he took her hand, lifted it to his lips and kissed it.

"Come on, Savannah. Think of all I've told you about me these past days."

It was true. He'd regaled her with stories about his family, about growing up in a big, glitzy hotel.

"Compared to yours, my life story's dull."

"Nothing about you could be dull." Sean kissed her fingers, one by one. "I want to know everything."

She looked at him. "Do you think your family will ask you detailed questions about me?"

"My fam…" Of course. She thought he was asking because the answers would help him maintain the fiction that they were getting married. Truth was, he'd damned near forgotten that was the reason they were here. "You never know," he said, hoping he sounded sincere. "What am I gonna do when Keir asks if you got straight A's in school, or Cull wants to know if you were a Girl Scout?" He tapped the tip of her nose with his finger. "Some things are very important to the O'Connell clan."

For a second, she thought he was serious. Then he grinned, reached for her and hauled her into his lap.

"I'll bet you did get straight A's."

She had, for a while. When her mother was still alive, and even the two years in that first foster home, before the man she was supposed to call Daddy started noticing her budding breasts, and the woman she'd never been able to call Mom realized he was noticing.

"Savannah?" Sean kissed her mouth. "Hey," he said softly, "I'm only teasing. You don't have to tell me anything you don't want to tell me."

"No. You're right. You need to know more about me."

The look in her eyes made him sorry he'd raised the subject. "I don't," he said fiercely. "I'm going to be introducing you as the woman I love. Nobody's going to have the right to question either of us."

Savannah's heart skipped a beat. "As the woman you'll be pretending to love," she said carefully.

Their eyes met. "Yeah," he said, after a minute. "That's what I meant."

An honest answer from an honest man. She couldn't ask for anything more, could she? At the very least, he deserved honesty in return.

"Well," she said slowly, "I was never a Girl Scout..."

She told him everything. About her father, who'd left when she was so small she couldn't remember him. About her mother, a drug addict, and how she'd died.

She told him about her sister, cruelly disabled by an illness no one really understood, and how Missy had screamed and screamed when the authorities separated them and put

Savannah in the first of a series of foster homes and Missy in an institution.

She told him how she'd hated those homes, though she left out the uglier details, and how she'd run away from the last and worst one, how she'd found a way to snatch Missy, how they'd hitchhiked from Savannah—the city her mother had named her for—to New Orleans. How they'd survived with her earning money using skills she'd picked up and honed in one of the endless series of foster homes.

She told him all the things she'd never told anyone, and by the time she talked of Alain, how he'd rescued her and Missy, how she'd thought he was her savior, she was weeping, the sound so raw and heartbreaking, Sean cursed the fates that had kept him from finding her sooner.

"Hush," he said, as he lifted her tearstained face to his and kissed her and kissed her until the world was reduced to only the two of them. Only the two of them, because only the two of them mattered.

That was the minute when he knew that he loved her.

HE TOLD HER THAT NIGHT.

It was their last on the island. The next afternoon, they would fly to Las Vegas. He'd thought he'd tell her there. Or maybe on the plane. He'd wait a little while, until the time was right.

But walking hand in hand along the beach, under the benevolent gaze of a fat, ivory moon, he suddenly knew it would never be more right than this. He'd never felt more vulnerable in his life as he turned her toward him.

"Savannah," he said. "Savannah…"

She raised her face to his, and when he looked into her eyes, he saw something that told him everything would be all right.

"Savannah," he said softly, smiling with wonder, "you're in love with me."

She jerked under his hands. "My God, O'Connell, you have the most monumental ego—"

Sean lifted her to her toes and kissed her. "You'd better be in love with me," he whispered against her mouth, "because I love you. I adore you. You hear me, Just-Savannah? I love you with all my heart."

Time seemed to stop. Nothing moved, not the sea or the air or Savannah. Sean felt a chill in his blood. Maybe he was wrong. Maybe she didn't feel what he did. Maybe—

And then she gave a little cry and threw her arms around him.

They made love there, on the still-warm sand, and then he carried her to the house and they made love in the shower. They went to bed and slept curled together, and when they awoke before dawn, they made love again.

"I love you," Savannah whispered, looking up at him, her eyes wide with wonder as he slipped deep, deep inside her. "I love you, love you, love—"

He kissed her and they flew, together, into the blinding white heat of the universe.

CHAPTER THIRTEEN

SAVANNAH DIDN'T WANT to leave their house or their island.

That was how she'd come to think of this place where she and Sean had forged their love. They were safe here. They belonged here.

Heaven only knew what the real world had in store.

Boarding the jet for their flight to Las Vegas, her teeth were all but chattering. Sean kept his arm tightly around her and hugged her to his side.

"There's nothing to worry about. My family's going to love you."

She nodded, as if she believed him, but she didn't. Those brothers he always talked about sounded just like him. Big. Strong. Smart. They'd see right through her, know in an instant she didn't measure up to their wives who were undoubtedly women from good, solid backgrounds—backgrounds that were nothing like hers.

And his sisters... She could almost see them. Bright. Beautiful. Proper. One single, two married to men who were so powerful it made her head spin. Fallon's husband was head of an international conglomerate. Megan's was a sheikh.

A sheikh! she thought, and bit back hysterical laughter.

And then there was Sean's mother. Mary Elizabeth O'Connell-Coyle. The matriarch of the clan. Sean adored her—that was obvious. What son wouldn't adore a woman who sounded like a cross between a queen and a saint?

You couldn't leave his stepfather out of the equation. His name, Sean told her, was Daniel. He'd been a cop. Cops always made her nervous, ever since her days on the streets. They saw right through a person. It would take Dan Coyle five seconds to know what she really was, just a dirty-faced street kid who was about to pull the biggest scam of her life on some very nice people who deserved better.

She told herself it wasn't a complete scam. She wasn't Sean's wife but they were in love. They'd only be stretching the truth a little.

Who was she kidding? They'd be stretching it a lot.

The money. She had to concentrate on the money, though thinking about it was agony. She had to take it. With it, she could save her sister's life—but Sean didn't know that. She hadn't told him about Alain's threats, not just to Missy but to her. That he'd intended to use her as a prize.

She couldn't risk telling Sean. He despised Alain already. She was afraid of what he might do if he knew the true extent of Alain's villainy. Not that she gave a damn about Alain. It was Sean she was worried about.

If he went after Alain because of her, if he hurt him, got in trouble, she'd never forgive herself.

The plane was airborne. Savannah shut her eyes and told herself she had no choice. She had to do this. Had to take the money. The money. The money...

Oh God!

How could she accept money from her lover? How could she lie to his family? She couldn't, that was all. End of story. She'd find another way.

"Sean," she whispered frantically, as their plane leveled off. "I can't do this!"

Sean took her hand. "Sure you can."

"Lying to all those people...? I don't know why we ever thought it would work."

He didn't answer, not for what seemed a long time. Then he nodded. "You're right," he said calmly. "It wouldn't."

She stared at him. "Then, what are we doing? Why are we going to this party?"

"We're going because it's my mother's birthday."

"But you just said—"

"And because I made her a promise."

"O'Connell, are you crazy? Two seconds ago, you and I agreed that—"

"That lying to my family would be a mistake." Sean undid his seat belt. Slowly and deliberately, he undid hers and drew her to him. In the hushed darkness of the first-class cabin, they might as well have been alone. "So we're not going to lie." He took a deep, deep breath. "You're wearing my ring." He reached into his pocket and took out the matching wedding band. "I want you to wear this, too."

Savannah looked at the band glittering in his palm. It was beautiful but it was as meaningless as the diamond winking on her left hand. Seeing it made her want to weep.

"I won't put it on. This is wrong, Sean. Don't you feel guilty? This is your family! You love them. How could I—how could we—"

"I do love them." He put his hand under her chin and tilted her face to his. "But I love you in a way I never imagined I could love anyone." Another deep breath. Hell, it was a good thing he was sitting. He'd spent the whole day thinking about this. He knew what he wanted. Nothing would change that. Then, how come his knees were knocking together? "Savannah McRae, will you be my wife?"

She stared at him in shock. "What?"

"Marry me as soon as we get to Vegas. I don't want to wait. We've waited too long as it is." His hands tightened on her shoulders. "I adore you, Savannah. I want to spend my life with you. I'll make you happy, I swear it. Are you worried about what this will do to your sister? Don't, sweetheart. We'll bring her to live with us. Or move her where she can get the best treatment.'' His voice grew rough. ''Damn it, Just-Savannah, say something!''

Savannah's eyes filled with tears, but they were the kind he'd prayed he'd see.

''Yes,'' she said, ''oh, yes, yes—''

He didn't let her say anything more. His mouth was already on hers.

THE WEDDING CEREMONY didn't take very long, but it was perfect.

Sean bought her a dozen pink roses, held her hand tightly in his while they took their vows.

''I love you with all my heart,'' he said once they were man and wife, and Savannah smiled into his eyes and kissed him.

His family had already gathered by the time they arrived at the Desert Song Hotel. The party wasn't until the next night, but they wanted some time alone together.

They were just what Savannah had expected they'd be.

They were nothing like she'd expected they'd be.

But they definitely were stunned when Sean drew her forward and introduced her as his wife. Nobody moved, nobody said a word. Then Mary Elizabeth laughed and kissed her on both cheeks.

''My son made me a promise,'' she said, and shot a sly look at Sean. ''And he's a man who keeps his promises. Welcome, Savannah. It's lovely meeting a new O'Connell.''

They all surrounded her then. His sisters, who weren't proper or stuffy at all. His sisters-in-law, who were as down to earth as they could be. His brothers-in-law, who could have been two nice men from anywhere instead of the billionaires they were. Dan, his stepfather, hugged her and said it was remarkable how he kept gaining new daughters.

Only his brothers seemed a little reserved.

They were polite and welcomed her to the fold. But all that evening, all the next day, she caught them checking her out with quick glances. Looking at each other in a way that was disconcerting.

"Is this for real?" she heard the one named Keir mutter to the one named Cullen.

Was what for real? What did they know?

Savannah told herself it didn't matter. She had Sean. He loved her. She loved him. What could possibly hurt her now?

THE ANSWER CAME in a phone call an hour before the big party. The family, all but Mary Elizabeth, was gathered in the living room.

"We told her she has to make an entrance," Megan said. "Actually, we arranged for a big surprise."

Fallon nodded. "One of the guests is a singer Ma adores. The second she steps into the room, he's going to launch into *Happy Birth—*"

"Savannah?" Bree was coming toward them with the phone in her hand. "Sorry to interrupt, guys, but there's a call for Savannah."

"For me? Are you sure? Nobody knows I'm here."

Bree smiled and handed her the phone. "Somebody does."

Savannah put the phone to her ear. "Hello, *chérie*," Alain said softly.

She felt the blood drain from her head. She looked around her, half-afraid he might be in the room. Sean caught her eye. *Something?* he mouthed. She forced a smile and shook her head. "Just a last minute—a last minute gift I ordered for your mother," she said, and went out on the terrace. She slid the door shut and took a deep breath. "What do you want, Alain?"

"Only what you were supposed to do a month ago, *chérie*. The public humiliation of Sean O'Connell."

She closed her eyes. "That's not going to happen."

"Ah, but it will, Savannah. And I'm indebted to you for setting things up so nicely." He chuckled. "A big family gathering, lots of important guests arriving from all parts of the globe..."

"How do you know all this?"

"I know everything, *chérie,* including the fact that you will do as you're told."

"No." Savannah clutched the terrace railing with her free hand. "Whatever you want, I won't do it. Do you understand, Alain? Everything has changed."

"Not everything," he said with a soft laugh she knew she'd never forget. There was a brief silence and then she heard a sound that almost drove her to her knees.

Her sister's incoherent weeping.

IN THE END, it was easy. When your life hung by a thread, you could do anything.

Alain told her what to do, and she did it. *And don't disconnect,* he said. *I want to hear every word.*

Savannah went back into the O'Connell apartment. It was crowding up; the first early guests had arrived. A quick look showed her that Mary Elizabeth had obeyed her daughters and hadn't yet appeared.

Savannah offered a silent prayer of thanks. Mary Elizabeth's absence was the only kindness fate would show tonight.

There was a microphone at the front of the room. For the singer, for those who wanted to offer toasts...

For what Savannah had to do next.

She went straight to it. "Everyone?" she said, and when her voice quavered, she cleared her throat and said it again. "Everyone?"

Faces turned toward her. People smiled. Surely, she was going to be the first to offer good wishes. Sean looked surprised but happy as he came through the crowd toward her.

"My wife," he said, slipping his arm around her waist. "I was going to introduce her to you all, but I guess she couldn't wait."

People laughed. Savannah swayed. "Savannah?" Sean murmured.

She stepped away from him. "My name," she said in a clear voice, "is Savannah McRae."

"It's Savannah O'Connell," Sean said, with a little smile that told her he didn't know what was happening but he'd play along.

"It's Savannah O'Connell," she said into the suddenly hushed room, "only because—because Sean O'Connell thinks that the best way to keep a promise is to lie to the people he supposedly loves."

A murmur swept the room. Jaws fell. Eyes widened. "Savannah," Sean said urgently, "don't." He reached for her but she slapped his hand away.

"A year ago, Sean O'Connell cheated at cards and walked off with a million dollars that wasn't his."

The murmur grew louder. She had to raise her voice to continue.

"I know this because—because my lover is the man he cheated. And now—and now, he's cheated again. Sean hired me to play the part of his fiancée. Of his wife. He paid me five hundred thousand dollars to—to make his mother, to make all of you think that—that he's a good and dutiful son. He isn't. He's a liar. A cheat. He's a—a—"

Sean went crazy. He caught Savannah around the waist, threw her over his shoulder and carried her from the room. It was like the night he'd carried her from the *Lorelei*.

He'd been angry at her then.

Now, he wanted to kill her.

It took all his self-control to get her out the door and drop her on her feet next to an elevator.

"Sean," she whispered, but he didn't even look at her.

"One question," he growled. "Just tell me one thing, sugar…"

Was it all a lie? That was what he wanted to ask her, but what for? He already knew the answer.

"Get the hell out of my sight," he said, "before I put my hands around your throat."

His brothers were waiting at the door. Without a word, they flanked him and headed for the fire stairs. Nobody spoke through the long descent. Nobody spoke as they headed for a corridor behind the reception desk and the office that had been Keir's when he ran the hotel.

Cullen shut the door. Keir opened a cupboard, dug around inside and took out a bottle of whiskey and some glasses. He poured; the brothers picked up the glasses and tossed down the whiskey. Sean held his glass out again and Keir refilled it.

"Well?" he finally said. "Aren't you going to tell me what a stupid son of a bitch I am?"

"You're a stupid son of a bitch," Cullen said, but without any heat.

"Yeah," Sean said roughly, and tried to swallow past the lump in his throat.

"Was she the same one?" Keir said. "The hooker you told us about?"

"Watch your mou…" Sean's shoulders drooped. He'd

told enough lies, especially to himself. "Yeah. The same one."

"And you hired her for tonight?"

"Yes. At first."

His brothers looked at each other. "What's that supposed to mean?"

"I hired her." Sean hesitated. "Then I fell in love with her. And married her. And if either of you tells me again that I'm a stupid son of a bitch—" His voice broke. He saw his brothers' horrified looks and he turned away. "Listen, I'm going to go for a walk, okay? No, you guys stay here. I want to be alone for a while."

"Sean—"

"Kid—"

The door swung open. Their stepfather looked from one brother to the other, then set his gaze on Sean.

"I got a trace on that phone call your, uh, Savannah got just before she—I got a trace."

"Pays to have an ex-cop in the family," Cullen said with a tight smile.

"It came from—"

"A yacht off an island in the Bahamas." Sean nodded. "Thanks, Dan, but I could have saved you the trouble."

"It came from the Shalimar Hotel."

Sean stared at the older man. "The Shalimar two blocks from here?"

"That's right. So I called the head of security over there, asked some questions…" Dan pulled a notepad from his pocket. "Call was placed from a suite. Number 937. Occupants are one Alain Beaumont and a young girl." He glanced at the pad again. "A Melisande McRae."

It took a second to register. "Missy?" Sean said, staring at Dan.

"Also…maybe you don't want to hear this, son, but the

front desk called me, said there was a young woman sobbing her heart out as she ran through the lobby. One of our people went out after her, got to her just before she jumped into a taxi. 'Can I do anything for you?' our guy said, and this girl—blond and blue, five-seven, maybe 110—the girl looked at him and said nobody could do anything for her, that her—this is a quote, son—that her world had just ended and—Sean? Sean, you want us to come with you?''

"Let him go alone,'' Keir said softly, putting a hand on Dan's arm. He waited until Sean raced from the room. Then he flashed a tight smile at his brother and his stepfather. "But I'll be damned if I can see any harm in us following him.''

VEGAS WAS WHERE he'd grown up.

It was easy to get to the Shalimar, easy to go straight through the lobby to the elevators as if he were just another guest. It was even easier to find the door to suite 937, knock and say "Room Service'' in a way that sounded authentic.

What wasn't easy was to keep from pounding his fist into Beaumont's face when the man opened the door.

"I didn't order room ser—'' he said, but the words turned into a terrified squeal as Sean kicked the door shut, grabbed him by the throat and shoved him back inside.

"Where is she?''

Beaumont clawed at his throat. "You're choking me!''

Sean slammed him against the wall. "Where is she, you slimy son of a bitch? Tell me or so help me, I'll—''

"Sean?''

He swung around. Savannah stood in the doorway to a bedroom. Her eyes were red, her nose was running, and he knew she had never been more beautiful to him than she was at this moment. He could see a girl on the bed behind her, sleeping peacefully.

"Sean?" Savannah said again, and he flung Beaumont to the floor like the vermin he was and went to her.

"Savannah. Are you all right?"

"Yes. I'm— How did you find me?"

"Your sister. Missy. Is she all right, too?"

"She's fine. She cried when she saw me…" Savannah's voice broke. "I thought I'd lost you forever."

Sean opened his arms and she flew into them. He held her tightly against his heart.

"It's okay," he crooned. "Sweetheart, it's okay, I promise. Everything's going to be fine."

"He took Missy. He said—he said he was going to leave her at a place. A—a horrible place…"

"Hush, baby. I'm here now. I'll take care of everything."

Savannah buried her face against Sean's throat, her tears hot on his skin. From the corner of his eye, he saw Beaumont rising to his knees.

"Don't," he said softly, "not unless you want your face rearranged."

"Sean." Savannah looked up. "Sean, I love you with all my heart. I had to say those things. Beaumont—"

Sean kissed her until he felt some of the tension begin to ease from her body.

"I know you do. I should never have believed any of that stuff you said."

She gave a watery laugh. "I'm a good actress, remember? You told me that yourself."

"Please," Beaumont whimpered. "Sean. Mr. O'Connell. This is all a terrible misunderstanding."

There was a knock at the door. "Sean? Sean, you in there?"

Sean grinned, reached back and opened the door. Keir, Cullen and Dan stepped into the room. They looked at

Beaumont, cowering on the floor, then at Sean and Savannah, wrapped in each other's arms.

"Looks like you need somebody to take out the trash," Keir said.

"Please," Beaumont whispered, "gentlemen, I beg you…"

"Dan?" Sean shot Beaumont one last cold look. "Dan, your pals in law enforcement might be interested in knowing how this man took a minor from a sanitarium without the consent of her legal guardian, and what plans he had for her next."

Dan grinned. "How charming. Mr. Beaumont, I think we have several things to discuss."

Cullen looked at Sean. "You gonna be okay?"

Sean nodded. "I'll be fine."

He looked at Savannah, too. "Anything we can do to help?"

"My sister… I'd like a doctor to see her, just to make sure she's all right. And—and if you would be kind enough to find a room for her for tonight—"

"A room?" Keir snorted. "We have an entire hotel. Come to think of it, Cassie and I have a room adjoining ours that would be perfect, especially if we arrange for a nurse to keep her company. That sound okay?"

"It sounds wonderful." Savannah laughed and wiped the back of her hand across her eyes. "*You're* wonderful. All of you. How can I ever make up for tonight?"

"Just keep making the kid happy," Cullen said, smiling. "That's all we ask. Right, BB?"

Keir rolled his eyes. "You call me Big Brother again, pal, you're in trouble."

The brothers grinned, grabbed Beaumont by the arms and hauled him from the room. Dan was already on his cell phone, making arrangements with the district attorney.

"We'll send a car for you," Cullen called over his shoulder.

Once they were alone, Sean did his best to look serious. "Here's the thing," he said sternly. "You always have to tell me the truth, even if it's bad. That's what you should have done the minute that bastard phoned."

Savannah sighed. "I know. But I was afraid. I didn't know what he'd do to Missy. That was why I'd agreed to play you in the first place. Alain made threats…"

"Yeah," Sean said tightly, "well, those days are over."

"And I couldn't tell you. I was afraid you'd do something crazy and get hurt."

Sean kissed her. "The only thing that could ever hurt me," he said gruffly, "would be losing you."

Smiling, she looped her arms around his neck. "I'll never leave you, Sean O'Connell. You're stuck with me. We're married, remember?"

"Damned right we are," he said gruffly, and drew her closer. "And I've been thinking… A married man needs to settle down. Get a job—"

"A job?"

"Well, maybe not a job, exactly. Start a business. Hotels. Casinos. I'm not sure." He kissed her. "You'll have to work out the details with me."

Savannah laughed softly. "My pleasure, O'Connell."

"And I've been thinking about that ceremony we had this afternoon…"

"It was lovely," she said dreamily. "Despite Elvis."

Sean grinned. "It was, but, I don't know, maybe a once in a lifetime event should be a little more dignified."

"Dignified? You?" she said, but she smiled.

His arms tightened around her. "How would you feel if we did it all over again? The works. You in a white gown, me in a tux, my whole impossible family doing their best to drive us nuts... What do you think, Just-Savannah?''

''I think you're going to make me cry,'' she whispered.

''I'll never make you cry,'' he promised, ''except with happiness.''

Savannah raised her mouth to his and Sean kissed her until they were alone again in a world of their own making.

A world that would always and forever be real.

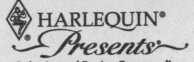

The world's bestselling romance series.

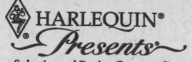

HARLEQUIN®
Presents~

Seduction and Passion Guaranteed!

Back by popular demand...

EXPECTING!

She's sexy, successful and PREGNANT!

Relax and enjoy our fabulous series about couples whose passion results in pregnancies... sometimes unexpected!

Share the surprises, emotions, drama and suspense as our parents-to-be come to terms with the prospect of bringing a new life into the world. All will discover that the business of making babies brings with it the most special love of all....

Our next arrival will be

HIS PREGNANCY BARGAIN by *Kim Lawrence*
On sale January 2005, #2441
Don't miss it!

THE BRABANTI BABY by *Catherine Spencer*
On sale February 2005, #2450

The world's bestselling romance series.

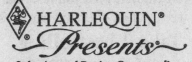

HARLEQUIN®
Presents

Seduction and Passion Guaranteed!

GREEK TYCOONS

They're the men who have everything—except a bride....

Wealth, power, charm—what else could a heart-stoppingly handsome tycoon need? In the GREEK TYCOONS miniseries you have already been introduced to some gorgeous Greek multimillionaires who are in need of wives.

THE GREEK BOSS'S DEMAND
by *Trish Morey*
On sale January 2005, #2444

THE GREEK TYCOON'S CONVENIENT MISTRESS
by *Lynne Graham*
On sale February 2005, #2445

THE GREEK'S SEVEN-DAY SEDUCTION
by *Susan Stephens*
On sale March 2005, #2455